BOUNCING TOWARD IGNOMINY

MILDLIFE MUDDLE
BOOK 3

SAM CHEEVER

ELECTRIC PROSE PUBLICATIONS

PRAISE FOR SAM CHEEVER

"You have that essential Je ne sais quoi that it takes to tell a story so mesmerizing you cannot stop reading once started. You are not telling stories to your readers...you are taking them with you on your adventures so that the experience can be shared by all as it happens and not simply replayed like a memory on the page of a diary! You are indeed gifted and it is my pleasure to read your books!"

Valerie Irwin

～

I was finally going to be able to stay on Earth to do a job. Joy of joys. No endless water dimension. No realm filled with slavering monsters. No dimension with deadly winds. It was going to be a piece of cake. Yep. I'm an idiot.

Ghouls. I was ready for them. Or so I thought. Justice and I had been working hard on my magical skills. The borders between dimensions had been quiet for almost a month. And I'd even managed to work my regular part-time gig at The Muddle, helping my best friend keep the human-type boogies at bay. But alas, the sanity was destined to end. And so was my naïve notion that working within my own dimension for a change was going to be familiar and easy. I'm such a putz. But then, what would you expect from a traveler who doesn't know how to travel?

STAY IN TOUCH

Sam doesn't give away a lot of books. But she values her readers and, to show it, she's gifting you a copy of a fun book just for signing up for her newsletter!

SIGN UP HERE!
https://samcheever.com/newsletter/

1

STOP TRYING TO BURY THAT ARM

"What's wrong with your face?"

I skimmed a quick look toward my best friend, wondering what had given me away. "Am I grimacing? You know I'm staring across the table at my least favorite beta male, right?"

Said beta male scratched his nose with a decidedly unfriendly finger. "Don't blame me because you look like you have shingles," Rog said. He pursed his full lips, narrowing his brown eyes on me. "Maybe you should get on a good antibiotic. People your age can't be too careful."

I fixed a hostile green gaze on my nemesis and said, "First of all, aren't you just seven years younger than I am? You're hiding more silver in that hair than a whole fleet of pirate ships. And secondly, I don't need antibiotics." What I did need was the ability to succeed and impress my favorite guide. Justice had been testing me over the last week to see how long I could delay a bounce without losing control of it. It only counted if, when I decided to accept the summons, I didn't flail and slam into the bounce at the end. I was on the razor edge of holding it for too long and I knew it. Unfortunately, Rog had basically dared me to give in and...well...let's just say that I'd rather eat a pile of raw seaweed than let him win.

Molly smoothed her glossy brown hair, which was below shoulder length and currently pulled back in a flawless ponytail. She narrowed a disgusted hazel gaze on me. "You're getting weirder by the day."

I barked out a laugh. "Says the woman who's been hanging out with a commitment-challenged traveler-guide named Juggler."

Molly's perfectly painted lips quirked in the corners. Seeing the potential for romantic sharing in the action, Rog and I sat forward in eager anticipation. But my best friend was no piker. She knew we wanted the deets on her and Juggler's relationship. Which was why she'd rather share that plate of bitter seaweed than tell us.

An irritated face suddenly filled the space between Rog and me. A face with sharp, chiseled features and deep-set sapphire eyes that were framed with impossibly thick lashes. I jumped slightly. "Traveler Kitt?" The voice held a challenge and more than a little impatience.

I pretended not to see Justice's delicious face, lifting my iced tea and sipping daintily. A huge, black paw emerged from the bubble in space and time and smacked my glass. It flew sideways, spreading amber liquid across the tiled floor and nearby diners.

Glass shattered in the aisle and I covered my head as determined drops of flying tea shot toward my short auburn cap of curls.

All eyes slid my way as I tried to sink into my seat cushion.

Justice and Elvo disappeared, dang their souls, and Molly leaped up, brandishing a linen napkin on her pale, pink suit. "What in the world is wrong with you?!" she squealed. "This suit is one of my best sellers."

What that had to do with my dribbling tea over it I'd probably never know. "Sorry, Mols. Justice is getting impatient."

She stopped dabbing at her suit amid annoyed grumbles coming from the table I'd doused, and lifted her perfectly manicured mahogany brows. "Justice is here?" She glanced around the elegant café as I mouthed, *Sorry*, to the people at the next table.

"Not *here*, here." I said, sounding like a drooling fool.

She stared at me another beat and then said, "Ah."

"Ah?" Rog squeaked in an unmanly way. "What exactly does *Ah* mean?"

"A statement of understanding," I told him, dabbing at tea on the tablecloth. "An expression of comprehension."

Rog scratched his nose again with the rude finger. "You guys are getting too weird for me," he groused. "It's embarrassing being seen with you."

I gave him a quick grin. "Good. Then you can leave and never accompany us again."

Something tugged hard on the front of my blouse. I jolted into silence, blinking rapidly.

A circular orb with visible stitches shot toward my face and I ducked. The projectile dissipated into nothing before hitting me. I growled.

"Maybe you have an infected chin hair," Rog said as he picked up a ketchup-drenched fry and nibbled it.

A second baseball missed braining me by centimeters. I spent the next few seconds dodging and dipping sideways in my seat. Backward, forward, to the left, down and to the right...the projectiles had amazing range for something coming through dimensional walls. I finally caught a particularly powerfully thrown ball in my right hand, wincing as it made contact with my palm before dissipating.

Molly lowered her voice, dipping her head and eyeing me from beneath a thick arc of lashes as if that would keep anyone from noticing that her mouth was moving. "Rae, you're acting like a crazy person."

I sighed. "Okay. I need to go to the Ladies." I stood up, glaring at Rog when he laughed. "I'll see you at the store in a couple of hours."

Molly's slender shoulders relaxed and she winked. "Give Justice my love."

I threw my napkin on the table. "I'm *not* doing that."

"Why not?" She actually sounded hurt.

"Because if he has your love, he won't need mine. Yours is much better."

She laughed. "Go get him, tiger."

Rog made a gagging sound, so I introduced him to my little friend at the center of my left hand. "Hasta le vista, baby."

The world wrenched sideways. *Oh, oh.* It twisted clockwise and then jerked back the other way. It was all I could do to make it to the Ladies' room before the bounce jerked me right out of the restaurant.

As it was, I was dancing and jerking like a marionette on a string with too many knots in it.

I landed on the pitch, just in time to scream and dive sideways to avoid being clocked by a baseball. I hit the orange dirt...what was up with the orange dirt?...and skidded several feet before slamming to a stop in a cloud of dust.

"Safe!" Justice yelled from the mound. He straightened from a pitcher's stance, his long form loose and agile.

I glared at him, trying not to notice how yummy he looked. Sitting up, I brushed at the weird dust coating me. "Very funny."

My guide strode over, looking all yummy and hot, and offered me a hand. "Good staying power."

I took his hand and nearly flew to my feet. The man was wicked strong. "Thanks."

"Too bad you lost it in the end." He tucked a strand of wavy light brown hair behind his ear, the sun-kissed strand having escaped a careless pony at the back of his muscular neck.

All in all, my guide was a yummy specimen of a man. A fact that I'd had only limited success trying to ignore.

"You didn't need to be so impatient. I was handling it."

Justice threw the baseball into the air and caught it without looking. "It wasn't me. We have a case."

My eyes widened. "A case?" Glancing around, I noted the giant Hellhound mix that was currently digging a hole to China in the outfield. Some poor sucker was going to drop like a rock trying to stop a home run. "Here?"

"On Terro, yes." Justice followed my gaze and sighed. "Elvo! Don't bury that arm there."

The shaggy, black hound lifted his head and tilted it in question.

"Arm?"

My guide inhaled deeply, releasing the air in a gust. "Don't ask. It's not a pretty story."

I opened my mouth, hesitated, then closed it again. Nope. I wasn't going there. "What's the case about?" I had a sudden thought and winced. "Please tell me it's not more of those giant rat guys."

He dropped an arm around my shoulders, tugging me toward Elvo, who was trying to shove something long and pale into the hole he'd made.

"Elvo!" Justice yelled again. The dog dropped his treasure, glanced our way, hesitated, and then seemed to give a shrug and trotted toward us, tail wagging and tongue flapping around his shaggy face. I braced for arm-flavored dog kisses. My hands flying out in front of me, I shook my head. "No thanks. I don't need dead arm cooties right now. But thanks for the thought."

The hound dropped to his wide haunches, cocking his head again, and whined as if I'd insulted his best friend.

That was okay. He could whine. "I really should probably ask about the arm."

Justice shook his head. "Don't worry about the arm. We've got a real mess to clean up here."

Glancing around, I frowned. "I don't see any mess."

Justice frowned too. "Oh. I forgot. Here..." He flipped a hand and everything changed. I gasped, stumbling backward. "What?"

"I cloaked it so nobody could see the mess."

My heels hit something dense and kind of squishy. I jerked away with a squeal and hit something else that was even squishier. I ping-ponged away on a scream and nearly went down in a pile of body parts, some of which had gone well past their freshness date. Justice caught me before I fell and Elvo bounced happily, barking as I tried to climb my partner to keep from touching anything.

Grunting, Justice shifted his weight to hold me over one shoulder in a combination drunk girl transport of shame and pseudo fireman's carry. "This isn't very manly behavior," he ground out, obvious strain in his sexy voice as he struggled to hold me in the awkward clutch.

"Why are there millions of slimy body parts all over this field?"

"Your guess is as good as mine," he said, trying to shift me into a more comfortable position. For him. Not me. The new position put one of his firmly muscled shoulders squarely into my gut. "But I'm guessing it might have something to do with the chomp of ghouls that escaped Igne last night."

I tried to shift to move his pointy shoulder out of my stomach, nearly taking us both down to the part-strewn ground in the process. "A *chomp* of ghouls?"

He grinned. "As far as I know there isn't a term for a group of the things. So, I made one up."

I sighed.

"I'm putting you down now, Rae."

"No!" I clutched desperately at him, managing to nearly strangle him in an attempt to keep from being set back onto my feet.

He grunted. "Man up, Traveler, or I'm just going to drop you and your landing won't be fun."

Ugh! "Okay, okay." I grimaced down at my pretty red sneakers. They were brand new. "Can I borrow your boots?"

He eyed my sneakers and gave me a flat look. "You want me to give you my boots? Then what do I wear?"

"You'd look really good in red."

"I don't do pink, polka-dotted bows, Traveler."

"But these are brand new," I whined.

Elvo cocked his head and glanced at my sneakers. Before I knew what he was doing, he'd lumbered over and licked them from toe to heel, coating my pretty new shoes in dog spit tinged with something I didn't want to identify.

"There," Justice said. "They're already ruined. You might as well trudge through some body parts in them."

I growled a little. "Retirement was supposed to be fun and easy and dog-spit free."

"Good thing you're not retired then," my guide said, sliding me to the ground. "That sounds really boring."

"Whoof!" agreed Elvo.

2

EVERYTHING ABOUT THIS IS DISGUSTING

I grimaced as my once cute canvas sneakers splatted down in something that was truly disgusting and my stomach rolled unhappily as I slipped a little in the goo. "I guess there's no freshness date on the bodies these guys dig up?"

Justice was crouching down beside a relatively intact body, studying the mangled face with much more interest than it seemed to warrant.

I stepped up behind him and wrinkled my nose against the stench. "Studying to be a serial killer?"

He glanced up with an unreadable expression. "Come closer, I want to tell you a little secret."

I snorted. "Nice try. What are you looking for?"

He pointed toward a patchwork of small wounds around the mouth and nose. "See those there?"

I bent closer. "Are those claw wounds?"

"Teeth." Justice swung a finger toward the gaping hole where the heart and lungs had been. "That's from claws."

I nodded. "Subtle difference."

He straightened, looking around at the sea of bodies. "There's nothing subtle about these guys."

"Why the dump site? I presume they dug the bodies up in cemeteries?"

He nodded. "Mostly. This guy was a fresh victim."

"How can you tell?"

"He wasn't embalmed."

I grimaced again. "They chew on embalmed bodies?"

"They do. In fact, there's a theory that the embalming fluid keeps them young."

I snorted again. "Embalming cocktails? Yum."

He winced in agreement. "There's really nothing that isn't disgusting about ghouls."

We scanned another look around the site. I didn't know what my guide was seeing, but all I was seeing was a bunch of poor souls whose challenges hadn't ended with death. "What exactly are we looking for here?"

"A signature."

Justice started off toward a pile of parts. He waded through the mangled pieces of dead people as if it were a walk in the park. I'd been a cop for a long time...pretty much my entire adult life...but I couldn't have gotten to his level of calm acceptance in a thousand years. Dead bodies still spooked me a little. Probably because I'd once had a specter sit up from inside its body and give me a nasty look, as if I'd been the one to kill it.

A thing like that stays with you for a while.

Justice stood over what appeared to be a pile of armless, legless torsos. The skin around the joints was torn, as if the limbs had been pulled off, rather than cut. Around the torn skin were marks like the ones on the last guy's face. "These limbs were chewed off?"

"It looks that way." He nodded, narrowing his sapphire gaze thoughtfully.

Being a mature woman with a healthy appetite for male beauty, I couldn't help noticing how impossibly thick his dark gold lashes were or the chiseled perfection of his face and form.

He had light brown hair that curled at a muscular neck and appeared to have been highlighted from the sun. His strong square jaw featured a sexy goatee that blended into a short, light brown beard. And his body...sweet cherubs on a crescent moon...only a body like his could make a woman think about doing naughty things when standing in a field full of body parts.

"This isn't good."

I blinked, tearing my eyes away from the back of his jeans. Pockets. He had nice...back...pockets. "What's not good. I mean, what *is* good in this situation...but..." I flinched. "What's wrong?"

He stared at me for a beat, his gaze unreadable. "You're not getting an embalming high, are you?"

I shuddered. "I have no idea what that is, but... I'm definitely not. Getting that." Maybe I was.

He shook his head. "See that pile of torsos there?"

I nodded. "Yep. There's definitely a pile of torsos there."

"Do you notice anything strange about them?"

"Everything about a pile of torsos is strange."

His smile was slow and made my toes curl inside my goo-saturated shoes. "There's something even stranger than the fact that they're there."

"Stranger than the fact that you said, they're there?"

"Rae..."

I threw up my hands. "Sorry! I might be slightly

embalmed." I held my thumb and pointer finger up with very little space between them. "What am I looking for?"

"Tic Tac Toe."

"Is that ghoul humor?"

"In a way, it is. There's one particular ghoul who thinks it's funny to slice a tic tac toe game into his victim's bodies."

"That's disgusting."

"Yes. But. As we've established, everything about this is disgusting." Justice moved closer to the pile and crouched down again. He pointed to one torso's chest, right above where its heart would be if it was still there. I squinted at the spot, disregarding the random splotches of blood to find a small tic tac toe carving. "Ugh."

"Yeah. But worse than the reality of the carvings, is what this means for us."

"And what's that?"

"It means that we don't just have a few random ghouls illegally crossing from Igne to Terro. We have the king of all ghouls here. And, one thing you might not know about ghouls is that they're like honey bees."

My stomach twisted painfully. "Okay. You just ruined honey for me forever."

He shrugged. "Wherever the king goes..."

"The worker ghouls will follow," I mumbled. "Just ducky."

3

LIKE TAR ON A CAR'S UNDERBELLY

My phone rang as Justice shoved the massive metal gate of the cemetery open far enough to allow Elvo to slide through with us riding his backdraft. I glanced at the name on my screen and briefly considered letting it go to voicemail. I really didn't want to speak with the person on the other end while chasing a gang of ghouls across a cemetery at midnight.

Then I realized it didn't matter. My ex was barely better than a ghoul in temperament and manners. And I didn't really care if he knew what I was up to anyway. "It's a little late for a phone call, isn't it?" I said when I answered. In the seconds-long pause my admittedly rude question left in its wake, I had a terrible thought. "Is Elizabeth okay?" After all, one of the main reasons to receive a call at an unacceptable hour was because a loved one was in trouble. When he didn't answer right away, I said, "Tom? What's going on?"

"Ach..."

"What?" I jerked to a stop. "Why do you sound like you're dying?"

"Ahch..." Wet coughing filled the line, followed by a

gurgle.

"Tom?"

Justice stopped to stare at me, his expression unreadable in the low light.

I shook my head, feeling my nerves stretching taut. "Tom, what's going on?"

The line disconnected and I jerked around, my gaze slashing past Justice to the street. "I have to go. Something bad's happening to my ex."

Justice nodded. "Call if you need my help. Elvo and I will suss this out and you can join back up once you've taken care of your husband."

"*Ex*-husband!" I yelled as I took off running. "Don't forget the most important modifier."

The guide didn't respond and I probably wouldn't have heard him anyway if he had. My mind was already trying to decipher what I'd heard on the call. It had sounded bad. Maybe Tom was having a heart attack. The thought made me pick up speed until I was running flat out. I briefly considered calling our daughter, who was a nurse, and asking her if she'd heard from her dad. She kept close tabs on him since he wasn't the sort to take good care of himself. If he'd been sick, she'd know. But something kept me from making the call. Maybe it was the knowledge that ghouls were currently lumbering around our little town. And that thought had me digging in and running even faster.

I was fifteen minutes away from Tom's bachelor pad. An eternity in an emergency. And I couldn't shake the feeling that I was facing a real emergency. The man was a walking health alert, and he hadn't sounded good on the phone.

I slammed my car to a stop at the curb, wishing I'd been able to bounce there, but I hadn't mastered the trick of bouncing to unknown or non-assigned spots yet and hadn't wanted to waste time if I got lost. So, I'd had to bounce home and grab my elderly red Bronco. Cognizant of the lost time, I'd hit the nearly deserted midnight streets like a rocket, the car still rocking as I leaped out and reached for the gun I'd tucked into the waistband of my jeans when I'd left my apartment.

I hit the too-long grass with my gun down by my thigh, gaze skimming the area to take in my surroundings. I didn't question why I'd drawn my gun. My cop instincts were screaming at me that something wasn't right.

I glanced toward the staircase leading to the third level of the apartment complex and then to the window I knew belonged to Tom's place. Both were unnaturally dark. Glass crunched under the sole of my sneakers and I looked up to find the security lights broken and dark.

That explained the unnatural dimness in the stairwell. But Tom's apartment seemed darker than it should be, even at midnight. He was inexplicably fond of leaving lamps on in several rooms at all times. As the person who'd had to pay the electric bill, that tendency had been one of the many things about him that drove me crazy when we were married.

I slipped up the first rise of steps, dropping into my cop persona without a thought. My gaze was on a swivel as I climbed toward the third level, and I listened carefully for any sounds that would indicate a problem. The scuff of an unexpected step...a surprised intake of breath...a moan of pain.

The shadows around me were deep, clinging to the nooks and crannies of the ugly, clay-colored brick building like tar on a car's underbelly. My nerves thrummed with dread, years of experience on the police force giving me a really bad feeling about what I was walking into. That feeling was only exacerbated by what I spotted in the near distance behind the apartments.

A graveyard. Small and probably really old, the burial ground was painted in silver moonlight as if it were being highlighted by unseen forces for maximum effect. The stones formed slanting shapes in the distance that spoke of being long forgotten and badly kept. Given my earlier experience, I observed the graveyard more carefully than I normally would have.

Were the deep purple shadows there simply the product of the moon's fractured silver light? Or was there something more?

A thump behind the pale wooden door of my ex's apartment ripped my attention in that direction. My pulse spiked, my heart thumping hard against my ribs.

Taking a deep breath and slowly releasing it to calm my nerves, I reached out with my left hand and slowly turned the knob. The door came open with a silence that was surprising, given the age of the apartments and an obvious lack of upkeep.

I hesitated a beat, using all of my senses to gauge the situation I was walking into. The dread coating my spine deepened at what I discovered.

The coppery smell of blood.

The soft rasp of labored breaths.

An unnatural darkness filled with the cold of the grave.

And the sweet-sour taste of death that coated my nostrils and tongue.

None of those things boded well for my ex.

Needing movement like I needed fresh, death-free air in my lungs, I stepped forward, my sneaker lowering toward carpet on the other side of the door. The surface squished ominously as my shoe touched the floor.

A wet, sucking sound had my pulse spiking, followed by a horrific crunch. A low moan.

"Ugh!" I murmured softly. "That's just nasty."

Bone deep regret suddenly took my breath away. I forced air through my tight throat and stepped quietly into the shadows behind the door. I didn't love my ex anymore. Hadn't for years. But I would have never wished for him to suffer what I suspected he was suffering.

As my eyes slowly adjusted to the lack of light, I spotted a hunched form across the room. The thing's tattered clothing shifted with a soft brush of fabric against fabric every time it lowered its head toward the body that was stretched out on the rug.

I readied myself to move, suddenly realizing I'd forgotten to ask Justice how to kill a ghoul.

Sweet cupids on a crescent moon! I'd just have to wing it. I'd aim for the thing's head. Surely taking out its brains would kill it dead, right? Weren't ghouls like zombies? I didn't know. And that hole in my knowledge was bad.

Really bad.

I pulled a blade from its sheath at my waist and hefted it with my left hand. Two weapons had to be better than one. AmIright?

Breathing deeply and then regretting it as the horrible stench in the apartment slammed into me, I stepped out from behind the door. At first the thing ignored me. That was good. I'd move fast and, hopefully, take it out before it had time to react.

Best laid plans and all that.

I jerked into a run, gun drawn and knife held out to the side as I barreled toward the killer crouching over the body. I made it three feet before the ghoul straightened and spun, its movements liquid and lightning fast. I'd expected the thing to lumber and lurch like a zombie.

Not like zombies then.

Awesome.

It was inches away before I reacted. Its death-painted breath wafted over my face, icy and putrid. The monster's claws slashed the air a sigh away from my throat and one clawed fist slammed into me, sending me stumbling backward.

Then it was airborne, its tick-like body seeming to levitate for a beat as I threw myself into a bounce.

My feet touched down across the room and I fired my gun.

And fired.

And fired.

I kept firing the 9mm handgun until the clip was empty. The ghoul jerked with the impact of each bullet, but never slowed as it leaped toward me again. I bounced so quickly I didn't have time to pick my spot and I landed on top of the corpse on the floor.

"Ah!" I yelled, sliding off the body and stumbling away from it in an attempt to put distance between me and the ghoul.

It turned with a wet hiss and scarlet illumination glowed in its eyes as a random strand of light slipped over them. Then it sprang at me again.

I tried to bounce, but the thing was somehow there before I completed the thought. It slammed into me and I went down, the tick-like monster clacking overgrown teeth that looked like canine choppers as its gaze flashed eerie red light above me.

I slashed at its throat. Cold, thick blood splashed my face and arms, wetting my tee-shirt as I tried to twist away.

Teeth snapped near my throat. I slashed again, bathing myself in more of the monster's nasty blood but not caring. I was manic with fear. The ghoul was winning the battle and I was about to end up just like my unfortunate ex.

In a fit of pure desperation, I jerked my knee upward and slammed the bony part hard into the ghoul's family vault.

Did ghouls have testicles? I had no idea. But I was working on pure adrenaline at that point.

To my relief, I hit softly-padded flesh and the thing's head jerked back. It stilled for a long beat and then a high-pitched keening sound filled the room.

Pushing my hands into its heavy shoulders, I shoved with everything I had, desperate to get free. The monster was heavy, and moved barely enough for me to struggle out from underneath it and roll away. I leaped to my feet and spun as the ghoul started to move again. Leaping onto its back, I plunged my blade into its flesh with mindless fury.

Despite my dedicated attack, it easily got to its feet again, with me clinging to its back like an overgrown spider as it spun one direction and the other. The thing's clawed hands flailed the air in an attempt to get hold of me, but I leaned from side to side and managed to stay just out of reach.

"How can you still be alive?" I screamed in frustration. I was so busy trying to avoid the monster's claws and teeth that I neglected to worry about its other best weapon given our relative positions. Without warning, the ghoul's head snapped back and rammed into my nose. Cartilage crunched, crackled, and popped.

I lost my grip on the monster as blackness threatened and I hit the ground. I fell onto two bony legs and tried to get up. But the world was trying to smother me in charcoal feathers and I fell again.

One small part of me realized I needed to keep fighting. If I stopped, the ghoul would eat me like it had eaten poor Tom. I shook my head, trying to clear it, but that only spurred agony as my brain protested its recent treatment.

I fought to sit up, but dizziness held me in its sway. The monster's fangs snapped close to my face. Its graveyard stench assaulting my poor, broken nose. The monster's clawed hands found my chest and I wanted to scream. I was toast. The thing was going to break me open like a walnut and chew on my nutty-sweet interior.

I had to...

Light glinted off metal as a blade slipped silently through the air above me and the ghoul stiffened before slowly crumpling to the ground on top of me. A beat later, something hit the carpet beside me and I looked in horror at the gory, disembodied head on the carpet near my arm.

Groaning at the weight pressing me to the ground, I looked up into a familiar face and felt my world righting itself again. "Hey," I said to Justice.

His smile quickly turned to a grimace. "I hope it's him I'm smelling. If it's you, I'm calling a ride share to get home."

Elvo lumbered over and sniffed with interest at the fallen ghoul, tail wagging.

"Do you think that maybe you can pull this thing off me?"

Justice seemed to consider the question. Finally, when I was about to stab him in the leg with my blade, he nodded. "I should probably make you tell me the three ways to inca-pacitate a ghoul from the training manual before I help you up, but I've decided I can't do that to you."

"Gee, thanks," I grumbled. Back on my feet, I grabbed hold of his arm to keep from face-planting again.

Justice checked out my nose, which was bleeding copiously and throbbing like crazy. It felt as big as the hound's snout. "That's going to hurt in the morning."

"It hurts now," I complained.

He grinned. "You'll be fine."

"Why are you looking so happy?"

He shrugged, picking up the gun I'd dropped and handing it to me. "You can disable a ghoul by cutting off their heads, stabbing them in their most tender part, or slicing off an ear."

I let my eyes go wide. "An ear? Really?"

Justice nodded, bending toward the lamp nearest him. He turned the lamp on. Light flared like a supernova through the room. "They have a large vein that runs behind their ears. They'll bleed out within seconds if you slice that vein. In a pinch you can box their ears too. That won't extinguish them, but it will slow them down so you *can* kill them."

Shaking my head, I turned slowly around and forced myself to look at the body on the floor. Surprise and horror jolted me. "What in the world?" I'd expected to find my ex's mangled body lying on the floor, but what I was looking at was a woman. "I don't understand."

"What's wrong?" Justice asked.

I shook my head. "Maybe she's his girlfriend?" I quickly searched the rest of the apartment, finding it empty and strangely infused with pink, flowery fabrics. "Why is this random woman here?" I was mumbling to myself like a crazy woman, feeling confused.

"Whose girlfriend?" Justice asked, looking increasingly concerned by my behavior.

"Tom's."

"Who's Tom?"

I turned to him, blinking rapidly as I tried to work out

what was going on. Then it hit me. "Maybe they dragged him out to that graveyard."

Justice frowned. "Rae, take a deep breath. What are you burbling about?"

"This apartment belongs to my ex-husband. As you know, he called me when we were at the cemetery. He was... gurgling. I ran over here expecting to find him eaten."

"By a ghoul?"

I gave him a flat look. "Unless a lion escaped from the zoo, yes. What else would eat him?"

He bobbled his head. "Off the top of my head, there are over a dozen magical creatures who eat humans..."

I held up a hand. "Stop right there. Are any of those creatures loose in Fort Wallace right now?"

"Not that I know of..."

I nodded. "Was that not a ghoul you just beheaded here?"

Justice frowned. "We're getting off topic. Why are you concerned that the woman is in this apartment and he isn't?" My guide's too-handsome face folded into an expression I couldn't really read. "Are you upset because he has a girlfriend?"

"No!" Even to me, my explosive response seemed suspicious. I couldn't explain it. I had less than zero interest in getting back with my ex. The very thought made me shudder and gag. But maybe...

"Are you sure this is the right apartment?" Justice asked.

"Well, of course..." I trailed off, looking around. "His is the one at the top of the stairs on the right."

"There are three levels, Rae. This is only the second level. Maybe he's upstairs."

Jeezopete! Heat suffused my face. "Oh. Um. Let's check upstairs then."

4

IT SMELLS LIKE GHOUL IN HERE

Tom's door was open, the interior quiet. Only moonlight filled the room as I stepped inside. I held my gun and blade in front of me as I took in the space. A small upholstered chair lay on its side and the coffee table sagged down the middle, fractured into two large pieces. The floor was littered with broken picture frames, jagged chunks of ceramic, torn fabric, and mail that had likely been flung off the surface of the broken desk near the window.

Using my phone light, I spotted a single slash of blood on the wall alongside an arched opening leading to a hallway. My heart, which had been beating like an entire percussion section, slowed its frantic march when I saw no ravaged body on the rug. I wrinkled my nose when I slipped into the small kitchen, which was separated from the living room by a two-level countertop with a single stool.

The sour smell of old garbage wafted over me as I moved into the room, and my feet stuck to the wavy linoleum as I searched every cranny where a body could hide.

The pantry held a few canned items but no corpse. A closet with louvered doors contained a stacked washer and dryer, along with a pair of muddy boots and a few coats on a short rack.

"It smells like ghoul in here," Justice said.

I grimaced. "Maybe. Or it could be..." I opened the small washer and a sour stench wafted out at me. "...sour clothing that's been forgotten in the washer." I slammed the door closed again.

"That's part of it," Justice said, grimacing with me. "But there's definitely a tinge of ghoul in this apartment." He pointed toward the living room. "Something did all that."

A deep, goosebump-inducing bark drew us down the hall to the bedroom, which smelled more like dirty laundry than ghoul. Elvo had his nose buried in a pile of clothes in the open closet. "Ugh! Get your nose out of Tom's dirty socks," I grimaced, walking over to tug on Elvo's ruff when he didn't respond. Loud snuffling noises met my attempts to tug him out. "Come on..." I started to say as Elvo's big head came up and his tail began to wag. "Ah!" I stumbled back with a yelp. The hound was holding a human hand in his jaws.

My first thought was that we'd found Tom. Then I took a look at the disgusting body part. It was wearing nail polish. "That's not Tom," I told Justice as he joined us.

"That woman downstairs was missing a hand." He shoved past Elvo and started digging through the nasty pile of clothing.

"I hope you've had your tetanus shot," I told him.

Justice reared back with a shoe. I blinked, fighting the urge to step away. "Please don't tell me there's a foot in that."

"No." He pointed to a slash of brownish-red splashed

across the toe. I expelled a breath. "That's paint. He helped Lissy paint an old antique five years ago." In just a small indication of how completely opposite we were, Tom still had tee shirts and sneakers from his college days, while I threw shoes out and got new ones if the laces were worn. Stained tee shirts didn't last long in my house either.

Justice threw the shoe back on top of the stinky laundry. "He's not here. Maybe he escaped."

"Or maybe he was never here?" I said hopefully.

"The mess in the front room says otherwise," he argued. "And the smell of ghoul."

Though relieved that Tom wasn't Hamburger Unhelpful on the living room rug, I couldn't relax until I'd found and warned him about the ghouls in his neighborhood. He and everyone else in the building, assuming they hadn't all been eaten, were in danger. "We need to check out the rest of the building," I told Justice. My experience as a beat cop was nagging at me to do a door-to-door check before leaving the area. "What are we going to do about the ghoul downstairs?" I asked. "And the woman?"

Justice followed me outside, our steps falling behind as Elvo lumbered quickly down the stairs. "Elvo will take care of the ghoul," he told me. "We'll call the police about the woman. They'll just think they have some new kind of sicko serial killer in the area."

I didn't like that idea. "We need to tell them how to kill the ghouls, in case they run into one."

He shook his head. "No ghoul would allow itself to be caught by a human cop. They'll be perfectly safe."

Except that the ghoul downstairs had let us catch it. I'd opened my mouth to argue, when fire flared inside the darkened apartment on the second floor. I took off running, wondering what fresh Hell was being perpetrated on the poor dead woman.

Just inside the door, I jolted to a stop as Elvo stepped away from the body, the ghoul's corpse little more than a pile of ash on the carpet. The disembodied hand was sitting on the dead woman's chest, which would hopefully keep Tom out of the investigation into the woman's death.

I also noticed a pile of spent casings from my 9mm. Glancing at Elvo, I scooped the casings up and slipped them into my pocket. I hadn't realized the Hellhound would police my brass for me. The big goof was a one hound crime scene cleaner.

When Elvo turned around to look at us, I made a small sound and swallowed hard. The hound's eyes flared with red fire and, as he held my gaze, fire rolled over his enormous black body in a fiery caress. But when the flames hit the tip of his tail they dissipated on a whisper of air. He blinked the fire out of his eyes and then chuffed at me, trotting past to go outside.

I didn't think I'd ever get used to that.

I glanced at Justice.

"No more ghoul," my guide told me, then he gave me a smile that made my knees wobble and my body tingle. It was almost enough to make me forget we were searching for bodies and nasty, stinky ghouls.

Not exactly my idea of sexy times.

An hour later, we'd spoken to everyone in the building who was home. While we couldn't exactly ask them if they'd been visited by any ghouls lately, I framed the questioning around the possibility of Tom going missing. When someone opened the door and didn't have claw marks ripped across their flesh, I assumed they hadn't seen any ghouls. More interestingly, most of the people in the building knew and liked Tom. In fact, one woman seemed to like him a lot. As if she'd had a relationship with him.

The woman, whose name turned out to be Peggy Sue Pearson...the snark just writes itself...readily admitted they'd been dating.

Given that she was petite, quiet, and softly pretty, that information surprised me a little. I mean...the woman was the exact opposite of me.

I was almost a little offended by that.

Unfortunately, she seemed to like Justice a lot too.

"When was the last time you saw Tom?" I asked, pulling the pretty blonde's gaze reluctantly from my partner for the fifth time. If I narrowed my gaze a bit when she responded, I could be forgiven on that basis alone.

"Thomas?"

I wanted to reach out and pluck a perfect eyelash from her face. "That's who we were talking about, yes."

Peggy Sue didn't have the sense to look embarrassed by her lack of attention. Instead, she giggled like a cheerleader trying to attract the star quarterback and batted the aforementioned lashes at Justice.

My partner grabbed my wrist and pulled it down as my hand lifted toward her face. Those lashes had to be fakes. Which meant the woman was a filthy liar. She didn't own perfect eyelashes...she was just pretending she did. That made her a liar. Right?

Work with me here.

Justice shouldered me aside. "Ms. Pearson, did you speak to Thomas this evening?"

She looked at my partner as if he were a triple-dip hot fudge sundae with caramel bits and sighed dreamily. "Who?

Oh, yes. Thomas. I did, actually. He knocked on my door when he came home from work and asked me if I'd like to cook him dinner tonight." She giggled breathily. "Silly man. He knows how much I love to cook. It's very thoughtful of him to let me do it."

I snorted. That sounded just like Tom. In fact, if I'd had any suspicion that he might have been turned into a ghoul, I'd know he hadn't by that fact alone. We'd been divorced for over a year and he still tried to get me to cook him dinner. "Yeah, he's a real sweetie like that."

The woman nodded, smiling in agreement. Her gaze swung to Justice again. "You two are cops, right?" She didn't wait for us to respond, her gaze locked on my partner. "Did you see Governor Treadcamp's press conference tonight? He said the Wasp Stadium was off limits for everyone. Something about an earthquake." She reached over and touched Justice's hand. "What's that about?" she asked in a breathy voice. "Should I be worried? I mean, I'm all alone here."

Justice gave her a pleasant smile. "You're fine, ma'am. I believe the problem is isolated to the stadium."

Peggy Sue stepped closer, her hand wrapping around his. "Call me Peggy, please. You look like a man who loves a good roast and potatoes." She fluttered those damnable lashes. "I make a mean sugar cream pie."

"Why mean?" I asked, just because she was annoying me.

"Huh?"

I shrugged. "Why is your pie mean? I prefer my pies to be sweet."

Her giggle was slightly hysterical. She took a step back as if she thought my crazy might be catching.

"Especially if the roast is *good*. Why would you pair a good roast with a mean pie?"

"What time did you see Thomas?" Justice asked, giving me a look.

"I guess it was around six o'clock. He gets home right at six every night. She wrinkled her nose. "Selling insurance isn't that exciting. He says some days he just stares at the clock all day."

I couldn't blame him for that. If I had my ex's job I'd poke myself in the eye with a letter opener just to escape the boredom.

Did anybody still use letter openers? If not, it was a shame. They were a two-in-one tool. They opened letters and could be used to poke bad guys.

"Rae?"

I blinked back to the present, tearing myself away from consideration of all things defunct. "I'm sorry, I was thinking."

His perfect brows lifted and I knew he on the verge of saying something snarky. To his credit, he managed to resist. "Did you have any more questions for Ms. Pearson?"

"Peggy Sue…" I smiled and she twitched as if I'd pinched her. "Did you hear any strange sounds tonight? Or see anything unusual?"

"You mean like that pony-sized black dog out on the landing?"

"Um, yeah. But not him. He…uh…belongs to someone down the street." I hoped she didn't ask me how I knew that. "Anything else?" I said quickly to head her off.

"It sounded as if Melly and Rob Johnson were going at it again." She shook her head. "Things crashin' and dishes breakin'. Those two are newlyweds. Only married a couple of months. At the rate they're going at it, they're not going to make it to their one-year anniversary."

I straightened at that, warning bells sounding. "He beats

her?" My right hand drifted toward where my duty belt used to be. I was going to cuff that jerk and drag him down to the station. Then I remembered I wasn't going to do any such thing. I was no longer a cop. At least not a human one.

Peggy Sue, eyes of blue, snorted out a laugh. "Beat her? No. I don't think so, anyway. I guess they could be into that BDSM stuff." Peggy Sue winked an over-lashed eye at Justice. I got the impression she wouldn't mind if he smacked her around just a little.

I didn't shake my head or roll my eyes, but it was close. "Thanks, Ms. Pearson," I said, handing her a card. "Call me when Tom shows up, okay?"

"Sure." She looked at Justice. "You got a card too, gorgeous?"

Justice avoided my gaze, his cheeks turning pink.

He was blushing! Oh smack. I was so gonna tease him about that.

I stepped outside first, ignoring Elvo as if I didn't know him, and waited until Justice closed the door behind him. I opened my mouth to tease him, and then he said, "We need to salt that graveyard."

My mouth snapped closed. "Must we?"

He threw an arm over my shoulders and led me toward the stairs. "We must."

The heavy clip-clop of the dog/pony's hooves sounded behind us, walking so close I felt hot breath on my calves. "We need to train your pony to carry me," I told my guide. "I'm tired."

Elvo chuffed and slipped around us, disappearing around the corner of the building and melting into the darkness.

"I'll get right on that."

"Good," I told him. "If you do, I'll bake you a mean pie."

"Only if you take the first bite," he said good-naturedly. "I want to see what a mean pie does before I eat it."

"Sissy."

5

ELVO SINGING TO THE MOON

The aged burial spot was surrounded by trees that were probably just as old as the graves and their crumbling markers. A soft wind sifted through the trees, making them dance and shake like costumed characters in a Mardi Gras parade. I shivered under the cool breeze, the scent of burning leaves in the distance not triggering my nostalgia button as it usually did.

Rubbing my arms, I looked around. The graveyard was small, covering maybe an acre of overlong grass and aggressive weeds. A feeling of sadness permeated the spot, and I couldn't stop the wave of melancholy that washed over me. "Okay," I said to Justice. "How do we do this?"

He crouched near an especially crumbly-looking gravestone, one hand resting on its fragile surface. I slid the beam of my flashlight over his handsome features, just as he turned to look up at me. A feral red glow showed in his deep-set sapphire gaze for a beat and I twitched with nerves. But the glow disappeared so fast I decided it had just been a trick of the light. I watched him as he stood, admiring his long, leanly muscular physique and the way even the moonlight seemed to caress his sun-bleached locks. He looked pretty darn good for a guy heading toward his three-hundred and sixty-sixth birthday.

"We salt the graves and the perimeter." He lifted the container of salt he'd retrieved from Tom's apartment. I held a salt grinder of pink sea salt that we'd borrowed from Justice's new heartthrob, Peggy Sue. She would have to be one of those cooks who thought regular old salt was beneath her. I eyed the giant-sized grinder and wondered how effective pink salt would be against monsters. It didn't seem manly enough for the task.

"Do we need to cover everything?" I asked, eyeing the grinder. "I'm not sure we've got the right materials to get it done."

Justice grinned. "Just sprinkle some on each stone. That should be enough. I'll do the entryways."

"You don't need to do the whole fence?" We both eyed the rusted, drooping fence line that looked as if it had never been repaired.

"Just the two entrances and any breaches. It might not look like much, but spirits and monsters can't breach a burial ground fence. They can only come through openings, and then only if there's no physical barrier there." Holding up the dark blue container, he said, "This is a barrier."

I nodded and headed for the stones that were furthest away from the rickety gate. I'd work my way forward as fast as I could. I'd always found burial grounds, especially the older ones, interesting. As a kid, I'd enjoyed reading the inscriptions on the stones and making up stories about the people buried there. I'd give them fascinating lives, making them pirates or adventurers of some kind. That game ended the day my parents disappeared on a trip into South America. They'd been hobby birders and had gone to the jungle to document the extremely rare Araripe Manakin. They'd walked into the jungle with a guide and had never come back out.

I'd stopped visiting burial grounds after that, the thought that my parents might be drying to dust beneath a jungle bush somewhere and I'd never find them taking the fun out of it.

I shook off the memories swamping me and tried to focus on the task ahead. Standing over an ancient tombstone and grinding pink salt onto its surface felt too ridiculous, and I hoped nobody saw me doing it. It would be hard to explain. Also, I decided I needed to start strengthening my wrists. I'd only done three stones and they were killing me from all the grinding.

On the plus side, my broken nose was only throbbing with occasional misery, rather than constant agony. So, there was that.

Hushshshsh...

I jolted to a stop, listening to my surroundings. Glancing around, I spotted Justice diligently salting one of the back gates. Near the front of the burial ground, a large, dark shape slid silently through the tombstones, red eyes glowing in the night.

Elvo.

I pulled air into my lungs and released it slowly. Whatever I thought I'd heard, it had been my imagination, or Elvo would have heard it too.

I went back to work, finishing two more stones. My wrists were screaming, so I stopped to shake them out.

Hushshshsh...

I jerked. Cold air sifted over me, bringing with it the sour stench of death or evil.

It was sometimes hard to tell the difference.

Stepping back from the stone, I spun in a quick circle, my hand clasping a blade as I took in my surroundings. An oversized stone stood straight and unblemished several feet away from me, the flowing script on its front surface unreadable. An angel crouched on its wide top, the eyes dark slits in the night.

My pulse spiked...heartbeats thudding against my ribs. The grip on my blade grew slippery as sweat bathed my palms. Pressure in my chest told me I hadn't taken a breath in a while.

Hushshshsh...

I jerked my gaze from the angel. Toward the shadows.

Hushshshsh...

I swung in a different direction, panting with dread. I fought the urge to call out to Justice. Somehow it felt as if my voice cutting through the silence would cause whatever it was to leap into movement.

Hushshshsh...

Behind me, Elvo barked. I started to turn. The night thickened and whipped into movement. I expelled a breath and turned just as the monster leaped, catching the ghoul in the throat with my knife. The blade sank deep, my knuckles smacking hard against cold, oily flesh.

I went down under the heavy form, my knee already snapping up to catch it in the crotch.

It had worked before...

I missed, hitting the spongy muscle of its thigh. Square, yellowed teeth snapped inches from my face, spitting sour saliva over my throat and chin. I either needed to give up on the knife or risk holding the ghoul off with one hand.

I wasn't giving up on the only thing that could save me.

Icy spit dripped over my cheek. "Gross!" I yelled, wildly grabbing for the blade embedded in the thing's desiccating throat. I managed to get my fingers around it, wondering why neither Elvo nor Justice had come to help.

My sweat-coated palm slipped off the grip.

The ghoul dug in its toes and shoved, trying to get its teeth around my throat. My arm trembled with the effort of holding it back. I wanted to scream for Justice, but there wasn't enough air. I panted shallowly, fighting despite knowing that I was inches away from a horrific death.

A howl split the night, followed by snarls and growling. It sounded as if Elvo was battling something near the front gate.

"Rae!?"

I couldn't respond to Justice's tension-filled call. Did he need my help? Or was he asking me if I needed his? Either way, it didn't matter. It was all I could do to hold the monster off. I grabbed for the hilt again and managed to get a good grip. The monster shoved forward, its thick, spongy knee slamming into my gut.

I seized as air gushed from my lungs and pain enveloped me. Wheezing frantically, I felt my hold on the monster weakening as I fought to breathe.

The ghoul slammed onto me, my arm finally giving out, Teeth grazed my neck and pain sliced through the touch. The teeth tightened, grinding against my flesh rather than piercing it. I realized with horror that the thing on top of me had to be a newly made ghoul. Its teeth hadn't yet turned knifelike.

Agony sizzled where the thing ground its flat teeth over my tender flesh. I had to somehow stop it, or I was going to die. And my death wouldn't be quick.

Finally managing to pull some air into my weighted down lungs, I reached again for the blade in the monster's neck. There was no room to yank it out. The hilt was pressed against my throat and the ghoul's weight was holding it in place. My only option was to move it side-to-side. Justice's instruction replayed across my mind.

Disable a ghoul by cutting off their heads, stabbing them in the testicles, or slicing off an ear.

The first two were off the table. But maybe I could get to the ear...

Elvo yelped, the sound closer than before. Tension ratcheted higher at the sound. My gut instinct was to help the big goof. But first I had to help myself.

Screaming with the effort, I dragged the blade sideways, cutting a path toward the ear. It was a large ear, sticking out from an oblong head with wisps of gray hair covering it.

The monster didn't react other than to chew with more determination on my throat. Warm blood slipped down my neck, wetting the neckline of my shirt.

That was bad.

I thought of bouncing. But as attached as the thing was to my neck, I was afraid it would just come with me on the bounce.

Gritting my teeth, I tried to ignore the indescribable pain and wrenched the blade sideways again. Thick, burgundy blood oozed from behind the ear, slowly easing down the thing's neck.

I was close, but I wasn't there yet.

The ghoul whipped its head from side-to-side and the teeth at my throat ripped a chunk of my flesh away.

I threw back my head on an agony-filled scream, fighting to throw the monster off me. But it had breached the barrier of my skin and it yanked again...white-hot agony slamming through me.

My vision blurred, turning the beast on top of me into a

shrouded nightmare. Its head nuzzling at my throat like a deadly lover.

My limbs went numb. My heartbeat slowed as blood rushed from what had to be an artery. Cold slipped through me as I fought to breathe. The hand that had been wrenching at the knife fell to the ground, and my sightless gaze found the silvery moon watching from above.

Dancing cherubs on a sled, I thought. I was going to turn into a ghoul. That wasn't what I'd had in mind when I'd thought about retiring from the traveler gig.

In the distance, Justice screamed my name. I wanted to respond, but words slipped away from me, washed from my throat on a river of blood.

The ghoul collapsed on top of me, its weight crushing my chest. I couldn't breathe past its squishy bulk. That was okay. I was dying anyway. The silvery moon faded away, turning its magical light to those who were still among the living. I had the irrational thought that the moon's magic no longer recognized me as I lay dying.

A charcoal wave took me under. The last thing I heard was howling...Elvo was singing to the moon. *Yes.* I thought. She still sees him. It was fitting that he would sing to her...

6

I WASN'T THRILLED ABOUT BEING A CHEW TOY FOR A BABY GHOUL

Putrid stink assailed me, the stench so foul it yanked me from my sleep. I grimaced. "Stinky ghouls..." I murmured, not fully awake. "Get away from me."

More stinky air wafted over me, warming my face as its moist horror coated my skin. The surface I was lying on bounced violently, my stomach lurching with the movement.

Something big landed next to me, a weight slamming onto my belly as the sound of panting invaded my fog. "Get off me!" I shoved the weight, an abundance of soft fur vibrating beneath my palms. My bed companion whined, dragging my foggy brain fully awake. I opened my eyes and found myself staring into a big hairy face, enormous white fangs framing the world's biggest pink tongue.

Elvo's tail swept over the covers. His huge form was mostly lying on top of me. Probably because the bed was so narrow. "Get..." I shoved him hard, and then harder as he resisted my expulsion technique. He lifted a few inches off the hard mattress and then sank back down, dropping his massive head onto my chest.

I groaned and sighed. Giving up, I dropped a hand onto his back and gave him a scratch. "I love you too, buddy," I said in a wheezy, air-starved voice. "I'd love you better if I could breathe."

A door opened across the room, the quadrangle of light it admitted bathing a sterile room that was almost completely white. In fact, if it weren't for the silvery sheen of aluminum tools and counters, the only color in the small room would be my visitor's frizzy orange hair and the purple bruises covering my body.

I lifted a hand in a wave. "Hey, Fair." Even to me, I sounded half dead, my voice weak and raspy.

The med tech's round, ruddy face creased in a smile, showing slightly crooked white teeth. Her chapped-looking cheeks and lips were not unusual in the dimension where the Traveler's Bureau was located. Aere was a wind-scoured plane featuring such brutal blasts of air that many of its residents lived in homes which were mostly underground. The place was light on trees or any kind of outdoor signage or decoration. There were, apparently, areas where the geographical makeup dampened the brutality of the wind. Those areas held the dimension's cities and towns, and presumably a few brave trees.

"You look better. Especially your nose. The swelling has gone way down. How are you feeling?" Fair skimmed a flat white device over me from head to toe. The tech kept her gaze on the device, carefully observing the data and then inputting information with fast-moving thumbs when she'd finished the scan.

"Like a five-hundred-pound Hellhound is sitting on my chest."

She grabbed my wrist to read my pulse before she realized I meant literally. Then she snapped her fingers and

Elvo dropped reluctantly to the ground. He didn't go far, though. Instead of lying down on the floor out of the way, he sat next to my bed and dropped his big head onto the mattress beside me.

"He's been worried about you," Fair said, giving the big hound a smile. "We tried to keep him out but he nearly took the door down trying to get to you."

Said door opened again. "I'm afraid that's my fault," crooned a deep, sexy voice I recognized. Justice strolled in and took up a spot next to Elvo. "I told him to guard you with his life."

Fair frowned. "Why would you do that? You know we would never hurt Traveler Kitt."

Justice's smile melted every female tendon in the room. Judging by the way Elvo was looking at him, he might have melted the dog's knees too. "He knows that. You're all still in one piece, aren't you?"

Fair narrowed her gaze and turned away, clearly deciding to ignore him. She patted my blanket-covered foot. "I'll be back in a few minutes with your meds. Don't get out of that bed. You lost a lot of blood and you're probably going to be a little wobbly."

I didn't tell her I needed to pee. My bladder needed privacy to work. I'd sneak in there and do what needed doing as soon as I was alone in the room. Wobbly knees be danged.

Justice waited for her to leave before saying, "You scared us half to death," he told me, grabbing my hand and lifting it to his warm lips.

Elvo whined in agreement.

"Sorry. I wasn't too thrilled about being a chew toy for a baby ghoul either."

He nodded. "I'm afraid that baby ghoul was bad news."

I swallowed hard, my throat still feeling sore and tight, and lifted my brows. "You just figured that out?"

Ignoring my sarcasm, he said, "Apparently, the ghoul king didn't just go to Terro for a graveside vacation. He's apparently there to make more minions."

My eyes went wide. "So, the fact that I was attacked by a fangless corpse wasn't just bad luck?"

"I'm afraid not." He frowned thoughtfully.

"Has Tom turned up?"

Justice shook his head. "Not yet. But you need to call your daughter and warn her to stay away."

The thought of that phone call coated my spine in ice. I'd so far managed not to introduce my only child to my new reality. She had no business getting embroiled in the world of monsters and magic. My friend Molly and her annoying assistant had been dragged kicking and screaming into my mess not all that long ago, and the outcome had been terrifying. They'd both somehow survived, but Rog had spent a lot of time in the very room where I was lying and Molly was currently dating a charming womanizer who all but assured a future broken heart. Said womanizer was both a guide like Justice, and a traveler, like me. A unique skillset that made him a valuable magical worker in the traveler universe. But it had also given him an ego the size of the globe and very little in the way of common sense.

Fortunately, Molly was much scarier than her five-feet-two-inch frame would suggest. If anybody could handle Juggler, it was my petite bestie.

"Lissy's a nurse," I told Justice. "She's going to see the outcome of these ghoul attacks. And she's going to have questions. Unfortunately, she won't come to me for the answers. She'll be worried, like I am, that she'll sound crazy." I chewed my lip, realizing that I might not be able to keep my kid out of the current mess. It would be wrong to leave her in the dark for a lot of reasons. But I couldn't tell her what was going on. I just couldn't.

"Maybe you should just tell her the truth."

I shook my head without even considering it. "That didn't work out well for Molly and Rog."

Rog had been visibly exhausted lately, and I suspected that had something to do with what I'd overheard him admitting to Molly. He'd been having nightmares about his experiences in the magical realms. Given what he'd gone through, I wasn't surprised.

Justice shrugged. "I don't know about that. Molly seems happy with Juggler. And that assistant of hers enjoyed having magic for a while."

"I guess so." I shook my head. There had to be a way to protect my family without exposing them to the crazy that had become my life. The worry made my head hurt, and I decided it was time to change the subject. "I need to get out of here. Why'd you bring me to the Bureau instead of to my house? I still have that magical healing ointment you gave me." I grinned because he knew I loved that stuff. I didn't have any idea what was in the little jar, but it was fantastic.

"The ointment couldn't repair the gaping hole in your throat."

I grimaced, lifting my hand to touch the spot and finding it smooth and warm. It felt like a bad bruise, but it was whole again. And I was alive. "Good point."

"You were a breath away from death," he said, his tone quiet and filled with tension.

I lifted my gaze to his, seeing the concern there. I squeezed the hand I still held. "I'm okay. Thanks for acting so quickly. You saved my life."

He shook his head. "You can thank Elvo for that. He

ripped the ghoul off you and let loose an impossible to ignore howl to call me over."

I grinned, patting the big, furry lug on top of his wide head. "Who's a good boy?"

Though Elvo wasn't pure canine, having enough intelligence to understand and react to human speech almost like a person, he was as susceptible as any dog to sappy praise and baby talk. His tail whipped into movement, whacking the metal legs of the small table beside the bed. The Hellhound mix bounced up and put enormous paws on the bed, apparently viewing my praise as an invitation to give me wet, stinky dog kisses.

I barely fended him off, only avoiding a wet face by blocking him with my arm at the last minute. "That's okay, buddy. You don't need to give me kisses. I know you love... ah!" He pressed his big body into me and got past my arm. "Help!"

Laughing, Justice grabbed Elvo's ruff and tugged. "Down boy. She's still hurting."

The big dog dropped to the floor on a whine, which I took as an apology.

I shoved the covers back and swung my legs over the side of the narrow bed.

"What are you doing?" Justice asked, his tone alarmed.

"I'm done lying around," I told him, shoving to my feet.

The world spun in a dizzying whirl and the floor fell out from under me. I plummeted toward the stainless-steel counter, only avoiding direct face-to-counter impact because Justice had really fast reaction time. He held me by the arms and lowered me back down to the hard, thin mattress.

"Stay in bed, Rae," he told me. "Or I'm going to have Elvo sit on you until you're better."

Palms up to head off further threats, I said. "Okay, okay. I'll just call Mols and warn her."

"Good." He eyed me. "Pinkie swear you'll stay in bed?"

I gave him a flat look. "Who'd you learn that one from?"

"Hey, I might be well over three hundred years old, but I pay attention."

I shook my head. "I'm not doing a pinkie swear."

He held up his fist. "Fist bump?"

I couldn't help it, I laughed. "Get out of here. I want to talk to Molly without you two goons staring at me."

Justice gave Elvo a short whistle and the big dog trotted after him and out the door. I waited until the door closed behind them before dialing my bestie. The phone rang five times and I was about to hang up when she answered. "Hey, chickie. You coming into work tonight?"

Tonight? I wasn't scheduled until the following...*Urp!* I swallowed a sound of horror. I'd likely slept the entire night away and more. There was no telling how late in the day it was. A quick glance at my phone told me nothing. The clock said, 0:00. Apparently time didn't jump dimensional borders. I was just glad that cell waves did.

"I'm not sure I'm going to make it, Mols," I told her. I'd tried to keep my tone light, but she saw right through me as usual.

"What's wrong? Did something monstery happen again?"

I winced. "You might say that." I sighed. "Listen, Mols. You're not going to like what I'm about to tell you."

"Then don't tell me," she said with her usual biting reasonableness. "I'm designing my Fall line. I'm in a creative bubble. A zero-negativity zone."

That explained why it had taken her so long to answer the phone. When Molly did her design work, she fell into a creative fog. Nothing pierced the fog. I was actually a little surprised that she'd answered my call. "Sorry. But I can't not tell you this."

A tension-filled silence came through the line. Then she expelled a long-suffering sigh. "Hit me."

I couldn't help teasing her. "Mols. You know I'm mostly non-violent."

She snorted. "Having seen you kill those bat-rastards recently, I beg to differ." She was, of course, referring to the nasty band of rat shifters Justice and I had battled in trying to rescue her.

"That was an exception..." I tried to say.

She cut me off. "And those giant chicken things..."

"Okay, that wasn't planned..."

"And that slimy mole monster..."

"Okay...well...that..."

"And Billy Stinkerman when he pulled my braid on the playground."

I harumphed. "Now, you know he deserved that beating. First of all, what's with that name? His parents must have hated him to give him that name."

"Billy?" more laughter.

"They must have wanted him to be wedgied, and wet-willied, and pantsed three times a day with that name. Besides, he made you cry. That right there deserves the death penalty."

A long silence filled the line. I figured Molly was trying to think of more times when I hadn't been anti-violence. She shouldn't have any trouble, since I'd been a cop for several decades. If I'd been known for anything as a cop, it had been my ability to snatch a fleeing perp by the back of his shirt and slam him to the ground so hard he'd lose track of what month it was while I snapped on the cuffs.

They'd called me Brain Bleed Kitt. A moniker I'd worn with pride.

"Okay, okay," I said when I heard the tell-tale snort of laughter on the other end of the line. "I'll own my flaws."

"*All* of them!" Molly squealed with delight.

Despite myself, I grinned. "Why, I oughta..."

She giggled some more. "Okay, girlfriend. As fun as this has been, I've got hours of work ahead of me. I'm doing an average protector series and I'm stuck on the pocket for my Street Sentinel slacks. I need to wrap this up and get back to work."

"Why don't you shape it like a holster."

"A holster?"

"Yeah, you know, so your sentinel can easily slide a gun into his or her pocket. I mean, if you're going with the warrior theme, play with the classics."

"Rae..."

"I know, leave the designing to you. It's a stupid idea. Forget I said anything."

"I should," she said after a beat. "Because I'll have to share credit for that little bit of pure genius with you. But I can't because I love you too much."

I grinned. "It's not stupid?"

"Are you kidding me? It's beyond perfect. Now, quick. Tell me why you called so I can get it sketched."

"Ghouls are overrunning Fort Wallace. Tom's missing, and I need to somehow tell Lissy to stay away without telling her why."

If I'd thought the silence on the other end was fraught before, I had to reset my understanding of the word. "Mols?"

"Do you need a beating?"

I sighed. "No?"

"You need to work up to stuff like that. Ghouls? Dancing

demons on Halloween, Rae. I swear to the goddess, I'm going to strangle you with my new camo scarf."

"You told me to make it quick."

"Since when do you listen to me? Besides, a girl needs to ease into the idea of ghouls." She sucked in an audible gasp. "Rog! He's going to pee himself."

"Speaking of girls," I mumbled. "What else is new? He could barely handle that animated PG movie about the haunted house last week. You don't think he really had to go to the bathroom all those times, did you? He was cowering in a corner of the lobby, drooling on himself because of the green, pie-eating ghost."

There was a sound that was suspiciously like a laugh on the other end of the line. "He had a bladder infection starting."

"Mmhm," I said. "Anyway, send Rog home and tell him to lock his doors and don't open them for anybody. These things kill people and take over their bodies." Or something like that. I didn't really know how the whole baby ghoul thing worked. My job was to kill the things, not study their habits.

"I can send him home, but I'm staying here until the Fall line is done."

"Mols..."

"Don't Mols me, Rae. You know my process. I can't be creative at home. I need to work here."

"Then call Juggler and ask him to come guard the store."

"I..." her voice trailed off. She'd been about to tell me no way. She wouldn't want him there because he'd be a distraction. But she caught herself because she knew I'd come instead. And I would be a lot less fun.

"Okay. I'll call Juggler."

"Promise?"

"Rae..."

Ignoring the warning in her tone, I said, "Pinkie swear?" Justice had poisoned my brain.

Molly snort-laughed.

"Swear on your Winter line," I insisted, knowing I was hitting below the belt. Molly treasured her Winter clothes line because for many designers, Winter clothes were a challenge to create excitement over. So, Molly being Molly, she loved the challenge and nearly always hit the high mark she set for herself.

"That's dirty pool, girlfriend."

"I know. Swear, Mols."

She sighed. "I swear on my Winter line that I'll call Juggler."

"As soon as we get off this call."

Was that growling I heard?

"Fine." She disconnected, and I felt only slightly guilty for raining on her parade. If it would keep her safe from the ghouls, I could live with it.

The door opened and Fair entered, the hall light haloing the bright wildness of her orange hair. She was holding three small bottles and an air syringe. "Are we ready for our meds?"

"Oh goodie," I said. "You're taking them too?"

7

YOU'VE GOT A FACE GOING ON RIGHT NOW

I bounced home the next morning. Or maybe I should say rolled. Whatever Fair gave me had left me feeling tired but pain free. Instead of giving in to my weariness by taking a nap, I made myself a strong cup of coffee and took a long, hot shower. A piece of toast between my lips and a travel mug of coffee in one hand, I grabbed my phone and keys and headed out to my car.

It wasn't until I stepped outside and saw the nearly empty parking lot that I remembered my car was probably still parked near Tom's place.

"Dangit!" I thought about it for a moment, considering calling a rideshare, and then dialed Molly instead. She was slow to answer again, but finally picked up on the heels of a squeal.

I pulled the phone away from my ear. "Hopefully you aren't being killed right now because I don't have a car."

Molly gave a breathy laugh and I got the sense it wasn't a response to my comment. "Rae? Where have you been? I've left several messages."

I glanced at my phone. Sure enough, she'd called five

times. "I've been...under the weather. Are you okay? Did Juggler keep you safe?"

A deep, husky voice murmured something in the background and Molly laughed breathlessly again. Mystery solved.

"He's there, isn't he?"

"Hi, Rae," Juggler said into the phone.

"Stop that!" Mols said. There were sounds of a scuffle, more laughing, and then Molly was back on the line. "Sorry about that. He's impossible."

The way she said it, as if the man was just too cute for words, made me want to yark. "Sorry to interrupt. I'll let you go. I just wanted to make sure you were okay."

"Wait. You said you didn't have a car. Where are you? I'll come pick you up."

"You're not going out alone," Juggler growled in his deep voice.

"Back off, neanderthal," Molly responded, a smile in her voice. "Where are you?" she asked me again.

"Home. Thanks, Mols."

"I'll be right there."

"*We'll* be right th..." Juggler tried to say before he was cut off.

I sighed. Had I created a monster when I'd encouraged her to call him? Hopefully, the man hadn't kept Molly from finishing her designs. She might be all rainbows with silver stars in her eyes at the moment, but when the afterglow went away, my bestie would become the crypt monster from the dark and deadly underworld if she was behind on her design schedule.

I dropped onto the concrete retaining wall behind me and thought about calling Tom one more time. Maybe he'd been on a hot date and hadn't gone home last night. Then I remembered I'd been out of touch for longer than that. I had trouble seeing Tom worming his way into someone's bed for more than the fifteen minutes it took him to complete his entire repertoire of sexual antics.

Still...

I dialed his number and it rang, and rang, and rang, and went to voicemail. "Tom, it's me. Call me as soon as you get this message."

My phone rang as soon as I disconnected. It was my daughter. "Hey, honey. How are you doing?"

"I'm okay. You haven't talked to Dad have you? I've been calling him since yesterday and he hasn't returned any of my calls."

"I actually just tried him. The call went to voicemail."

"You called him? Why? Is something wrong?"

I bit back a quick remark about her assumption there had to be trouble if I called her father. But she'd know better. I rarely engaged a conversation with Tom. If I did, it always had to do with Elisabeth. "I'm not sure, Lissy." I tried to think of something I could tell her that would keep her away from her dad's place and not make her think I'd lost my mind. I drew a blank. "He's probably just out of town on business and forgot to tell you."

"Without his phone?"

I winced. "Maybe the battery's dead on it. You know he always forgets to charge the thing." My ex didn't care for phones. In fact, he still carried one of those old-fashioned flip-phones that was dumber than a box of rocks. No smart phones for Thomas Kitt. He didn't need the competition.

"Yeah. You're right. So, what were you calling him about?"

Dangit!

"Um, I wanted to ask him about a charge on the credit card. Nothing earth shattering."

There was a stark silence and I braced for her to call me on it. I hadn't shared a charge card with my ex since about a month after our divorce, when he'd charged a bunch of stuff for his new apartment and then told me I had to pay the charges because I threw him out.

"Okay. Well, if you hear from him, will you tell him to call me?"

"Of course." I relaxed. "How's life in the ER treating you?" We chatted about her life as an emergency nurse for a few minutes. Then I spotted Molly's cute little Mini Cooper burning pavement up the road in my direction. The car fit Mols to a tee. It was petite and full of attitude, just like she was. "Okay, honey. I've got to get to work. Stay safe. There've been a spate of robberies in this area. You should have one of the cute doctors you work with walk you to your car after dark."

She snorted. "As if they'd know what to do with a robber. Unless the guy needed sutures, they'd be at a loss."

I laughed.

"Before you go, mom..."

I waved at Molly. "What is it, honey?"

"You're still connected to the cop rumor mill, right?"

"Sort of." I tensed, suspecting what she was about to ask. "Why?"

"Lately, there have been a bunch of DOAs with some kind of deep claw marks raking their torsos and throats. They look like animal attacks, only I don't know of any animals around here with claws like this." She hesitated. "Their hearts and other organs were missing, mom."

I closed my eyes and let dread fill me. If I'd had hopes that the ghouls were contained in and around Fort Wallace, her words told me they were empty ones. Lissy lived and worked in a lake community twenty minutes north of Fort Wallace. The area was remote enough that I'd hoped it would escape the notice of our newest monster mash.

"Mom?"

I realized I'd zoned out. Lissy had been talking to me. "Sorry, honey. Molly just got here to pick me up. What did you say?"

"I asked if you'd heard anything about this type of killing in your area?"

"I'm not sure. I'll ask around." I held up a finger for Molly to wait.

"Thanks. You don't think..." I envisioned her chewing the inside of her bottom lip as she tried to come up with the right way to form her next question. "Do you think it's some kind of serial killer?"

"I'd need to know more before I could answer that," I told her gently.

"I'll email you some records with the patients' personal info blocked out. Will you take a look at them?"

"Sure." I fought the desire to demand that she come stay with me. "But only if you promise me you'll have security walk you to your car tonight."

"Deal." She hesitated a moment before saying goodbye. I waited, knowing it was her way of working through something she wanted to say. Finally, she said, "Do you think you could drive by dad's place? I'd feel better if we knew he was okay."

I didn't hesitate, because it was an easy thing to promise. I needed to go back there again anyway. "Absolutely. I'm sure he's fine." Feeling like the worst kind of thug for lying to my daughter, I disconnected and headed for the tiny car idling at the curb.

Juggler turned around in his seat and eyed me. "What? You look pensive."

"Why do you say that?"

He floated his hands over his face as if to indicate my expression. "You've got a face going on right now."

I gave him a flat look. "Ghouls, Juggler. That's not enough of a reason for a face?"

He shrugged.

Pulling out of the parking lot, Molly asked, "Where to, Rae?"

"Tom's apartment. I need to get my car."

"You're not going into that apartment by yourself," she told me.

"It's okay. The corpses are gone. Elvo fired the ghouls." Our very own crime scene cleaner.

"That's not what I'm worried about," she said, rolling her hazel gaze to peer at me through the rear-view mirror. "You were a cop for like fifty years, Rae. I'm not worried about your reaction to a few dead bodies."

Juggler snorted.

"How old do you think I am, Mols?" I groused. "You do know you and I are about the same age, right?"

"I have a younger soul. It makes a difference."

Juggler bumped knuckles with her and made an explosion sound.

"Ah, so that's where Justice got the knuckle bumping thing."

"It's socially timely," Juggler said.

"I guess I should be thankful he's not asking me to slap him high fives."

Molly snorted. She turned onto Tom's road and sped up. "Juggler and I will go with you into the apartment."

I sighed, knowing she would dig in her heels and I

wouldn't be able to talk her out of it. "Fine. But if there's a ghoul, you need to run back to the car and lock the doors. Juggler and I will take care of it."

"What's the point of my coming with if I'm just gonna run away like a scared little girl when trouble comes?"

"Exactly," I said, sipping my coffee.

"Have you got enough of that to share?" Juggler asked, looking hopefully at me.

"Why didn't you make some of your own?"

"Molly's on a no caffeine kick. All she had at her place was chamomile tea."

I grimaced. "Mols! Are you trying to put the poor guy to sleep?"

"Not you too," she groaned. "He won't die without coffee."

"No," Juggler agreed. "But I'll feel like I'm dying."

I handed him my mug. "He'll be no good to me at all if we get attacked. He'll probably fall over from exhaustion and I'll be eaten."

Molly pulled up next to my car and stopped, cutting the engine. "That's why it's good I'll be there to help."

"Molly!" Juggler and I said in unison.

She held up a small hand, palm out. "Talk to the hand."

I stepped closer, pressing my face within an inch of her palm, enunciating slowly. "Hand, you are not going inside with us."

Molly gave me a tiny slap on the cheek. "Wrong again, Traveler Kitt."

I would have continued to argue with her, but a shrill scream tore through the relative silence around the apartment building, and Juggler and I were off like a shot.

8

YOU TOLD ME NOT TO TELL YOU

I took the steps to the second level in three bounds, following clumps and smears of dirt, that told me exactly what we were going to find when we located the source of the scream. Unfortunately, I recognized the apartment with the door hanging from a single hinge. Justice and I had been there before.

Juggler and I hit the walls on either side of the damaged door and readied our weapons. I left my gun in its holster and drew my blades from matching ankle sheaths beneath my jeans.

Juggler's blade was sword-length and I eyed him, wondering where it had been hidden.

Seeing the question in my gaze, he winked, mouthing the word, *Magic.*

I was never going to get used to that.

A second scream spurred me into motion. I ducked through the door and slammed into a wall of putrid, squishy flesh. The ghoul's stench swept over me like a windstorm, making my stomach roil and inspiring an involuntary shudder.

"We have a squishy," I called to Juggler. "Look alive," I screamed as I dodged the thing's raking claws, which were over an inch long, black, and sharper than they looked. Faster than I could react, the monster pinned me to the door frame and I was looking at a repeat of the graveyard incident,

Sharp, black teeth snapped an inch from my nose, and my instincts took over. The world shifted around me and I was standing on the decking between the apartments. To my horror, I was just in time to see Molly step into the apartment, a blade clutched in her small hands.

I bounced again, ending up in the doorway and charging through without hesitation. The dimly-lit room was filled with bodies. I counted at least four writhing, slashing, snapping ghouls as I took my first strike. My blades cleaved the first ghoul's head off its shoulders and it started to crumple. Unfortunately, it slashed out at me with its poisonous claws before it sank to the floor.

Fire burned across my skin where it struck. I spun away, slashing at the next ghoul as it charged me, teeth clacking and blackened, blistery skin sloughing nastily off its face. I could almost see the shape of a human face beneath the rotting flesh, but the ghoul's metamorphosis was too far gone. The human part of the creature was buried deep beneath a monster's poison.

I backed up under the attack, my blades flashing, and bumped into warm, firm flesh. Half-turning, I found Juggler fighting at my back. The ghoul I was battling took that moment to press its attack, rushing me and slashing both claws toward my throat. I ducked, bent slightly sideways, and came up with my blade buried in the beast's family vault.

The shriek that followed told me I'd hit pay dirt.

"Duck!" Juggler yelled and I didn't hesitate. A blade slid through the air an inch from where my head had been, so close some of my hair sifted downward to land on the carpet in front of me.

"Sorry, sorry!" yelled a familiar feminine voice.

I jerked upright. "Molly, get out of here! Are you crazy?"

To my shock, Molly stabbed toward Juggler. I yelped, but he lifted an arm and her blade sank into a ghoul just behind him. Expecting her boyfriend to yell at her to leave, I was more than shocked to see him grab her hand and whip her around so that they were back-to-back.

Molly was covered in gore and swirling like a banshee on steroids.

I caught myself staring, open-mouthed.

"Rae," Juggler yelled. "The victim."

Right. The victim.

I turned to find a wall of ghouls between me and the woman on the ground near the open refrigerator door. It appeared as though Peggy Sue Pearson had been searching for something in the fridge when she was attacked.

I envisioned the spot where I wanted to be and felt the air around me shift. The solid world drifted away for a beat and then returned as my sneakers landed on cold, slimy tile. Peggy Sue was blood-spattered and looking a little rough around the edges. But her chest was rising and falling, if a bit shallowly. As far as I could see, only her arm had been chewed on.

We'd apparently gotten there just in time.

I ducked at the sound of a feral growl behind me, dodging around a thick arm covered in flannel and spinning to look into an all-too-human face. Dull, square teeth clacked together and thick fingers plucked at a watch on the pale, dirty arm as if trying to figure out why it was there.

"Oh, buddy. They just yanked you out of the grave, didn't they?"

The baby ghoul stopped plucking at the fitness watch and narrowed its red eyes on me. The sound of my voice seemed to have surprised it.

"I'm Rae. We're trying to stop the king from making more ghouls. Do you know where he is?"

The mouth opened as if the ghoul was about to speak, but then he only clacked his teeth together. Apparently, the brain was too pudding-like to function.

I sighed. "Okay, I'll make sure you get put back into your grave. Okay?"

Something in the thing's eyes softened. For just a beat, the red in its irises bled away to a pale, pale blue. Moving as if it were being pulled against its will, the baby ghoul lumbered forward, arms flailing the air in front of me.

I realized he was fighting the imperative to attack. Maybe there wasn't so much pudding after all. I nodded and said, "I'm sorry this happened to you."

A single, bloody tear slipped down the ghoul's pasty cheek. My eyes burned with answering tears. Before I could change my mind, I slashed my blade into the flesh between the head and the ear.

The ghoul stared at me for a beat and then slowly fell to its knees. The mouth opened and I expected more clacking teeth. But to my surprise, he grunted out a single word. "Sta...dium." And then fell face first onto the hard tiles.

It took me a moment to realize the apartment had gone silent.

I looked up as Juggler and Molly joined me. "Did you hear?"

Juggler nodded. "I can't believe it talked."

"There was just enough humanity left, I guess." I wanted

to close my eyes against the memory of the guy's pain. "It was a heroic effort."

I stood, glancing around at the carnage. "We need Elvo."

Juggler nodded. "I'll find him." He headed out of the apartment, his long, sexy form shimmering into nothing before he reached the steps outside.

"My, my, my," Molly said.

I turned to find her admiring the spot where the guide had been. "Mols, please tell me you aren't falling for Juggler."

"Okay," she said, before swiping her bloody blade over the nearest ghoul's clothing.

"What does that mean?" I asked, narrowing my gaze suspiciously.

"Okay, I won't tell you I'm falling for Juggler."

I fell into step beside her as we headed toward Peggy Sue Pearson, whose eyes had just popped open. "You're not though. Right?" I hated the slightly whiny tone of my question.

"You told me not to tell you."

I might have growled. Just a little. "Mols," I said in a warning tone.

She finally smiled. "I'm not stupid, Rae. I like him. We have fun together. And he's teaching me to fight."

Relief tugged my lips into a grin. "Yeah. I saw. Impressive." She preened. And I smacked her upside the head. "Don't ever do that again."

Swiping at a strand of hair my smack had thrown into her face, she grinned. "No promises."

The air snapped behind us and we turned to find Elvo lumbering into the apartment, Justice behind him. The big Hellhound gave his bushy tail a quick wag when he spotted us, and then set to work extinguishing ghoul bodies. I flung up a hand as he approached my baby ghoul. "I promised that one I'd get him back to his grave."

"He can't be left in one piece, Rae," Justice told me. I glanced up at him, surprised. "Why not? He's dead."

"He was dead before. We need to destroy the body or the king will call him back."

Dangit! I thought about it for a minute, then held up a finger. "Hold on." I searched his pockets, looking for ID. There was nothing. But he did have a very distinctive tattoo, a giant lizard winding itself around his left arm. I took a picture of the tat and hurried down the hall. Stripping the flat sheet from Peggy Sue's bed, I brought it back and laid it down on the floor. We rolled my baby ghoul onto it. Nodding at Elvo, I said, "Don't burn the sheet, okay?"

The big hound chuffed with irritation. Apparently he didn't like travelers telling him his business. He was right. I had no idea how Hell fire worked. I only knew he was very good at wielding it.

"You're going to try to find out who he was?" Molly asked.

I nodded. "I promised I'd get him back to his grave."

"It's not going to be easy, just going by his tat."

"It might be easier than you think." There were only three tattoo parlors in Fort Wallace. "I could have one of my old buddies on the FWPD utilize tattoo recognition technology to look for it. I might get lucky."

My bestie nodded. "Good. Now, what stadium do you suppose he was referring to?"

Justice and I shared a look. "Could we have missed it?" I asked him. He shrugged. "They build their nests underground. Without digging up the whole stadium, we definitely could have missed it."

I grimaced. "I guess we're going back then." I crouched

and folded my new friend into the sheet, creating a bundle that would contain his ashes until I could get him back to his grave.

"Back where?" Molly asked irritably. "I swear, you two speak your own language sometimes."

Throwing an arm around Molly, I led her toward the door. Juggler was standing on the landing outside, his gaze focused on the street. Sirens screamed toward us in the distance. He'd clearly called the cops. "We're going back to where this all started," I told Molly and Juggler. "Hopefully, there won't be a sea of body parts this time."

9

A BALLET, WITH BLOOD

Fortunately, the Fort Wallace Wasps semi-pro baseball team's stadium had not returned to being a sea of bodies. If the ghoul king really had settled his nest there, he'd obviously rethought the intelligence of painting his hidey hole with bodies to make him easier to find.

Seems obvious, right? Nobody ever said ghouls were smart.

Elvo snuffled across the body-free grass, his tail down and his ears pinned back.

"Elvo can still smell the bodies," I said to no one in particular.

"Doubtful," Justice said. "Hell fire removes all trace. He's more likely smelling the ghouls themselves."

We eyed the spot where he'd stopped in the center of the outfield. Behind the pitcher's mound. "Please tell me we're not going to dig up Wasp Stadium," Molly said with a grimace.

"We're not going to dig up Wasp Stadium," I dutifully replied.

Molly sighed. "You're just humoring me."

I dropped my arm around her shoulders and gave them a squeeze. "I am."

Juggler, who'd headed for the nearest stadium entrance as soon as we'd arrived, let loose a shrill whistle and waved us over when we looked his way.

"Did you find the nest?" Justice asked as we stepped into the snack and ticket area, leaving the sun behind. The space smelled like old popcorn and overdone hot dogs, but not ghouls.

Juggler shook his head, his expression tense. He stepped through a door behind the ticket booth and held out a hand.

I followed him through the door and stopped with my hands on my hips. "What the...?"

Molly stuck her head through. "Dress up time?"

The small room was filled to the brim with racks of clothing. Men's suits, women's dresses, shoes, coats, and casual wear. The old wooden desk that was shoved into one corner was covered with wigs of all colors and styles, even men's, and accessories like purses and wallets. There were even some dated-looking uniforms that could have been used at one time for security guards and other law enforcement.

I stepped inside so Justice could come in. He frowned around at the collection of stuff. "This can't have anything to do with the ghouls."

"You wouldn't think so," I agreed.

Molly pulled out her phone and dialed. We all stared at her. No doubt the two men were wondering, as I was, who she was calling and why.

"Hey Gerald. How are you?" Molly grinned widely, then laughed as the person on the other end apparently responded with something witty. They chatted about unimportant things for a minute. Then Molly grew serious. "I actually did have a reason for calling. I'd heard a rumor that there was going to be an amateur fashion show at Wasp Stadium. Since it's post season, I was wondering if it was a fund-raiser."

She listened for a beat and then nodded, adding a verbal response. "I wanted to offer my help. I could even donate some clothes to the effort."

Her smile disappeared. "Oh? I see. That's too bad. No. I'll keep the idea in mind. I'll talk to you soon, Gerald. Tell Minks I miss seeing her at The Muddle." Molly disconnected. "No fashion show. In fact, there shouldn't be anybody in the stadium. Apparently, they've been having small earthquakes and the stadium is off limits to everybody until they figure out why the ground's unstable here."

"Earthquakes?" I repeated. "Just in this area? That doesn't make sense."

"I think we all know it isn't earthquakes." Justice brushed a hand over his face. "That explains why the entrances are chained."

Molly nodded. "Gerald said there are signs everywhere. Which we of course didn't see because you guys bounced us in. Nobody's allowed inside. Not even the city, until the entire space is tested for high resistivity areas. Whatever those are."

"Potential sink holes," I offered. "Air-filled voids that will probably continue to degrade." When everybody looked at me like I was from Mars, I shrugged. "I know things."

"Anyway," Molly continued, narrowing her gaze on me. "There's no reason all this stuff should be here."

"There has to be a reasonable explanation," Juggler said. "Maybe somebody who works for the Wasps is related to someone in a local theatre group and offered to store their stuff here off season."

We all nodded because that made as much sense as anything.

"Whatever the reason for this stuff, the ghouls are here. Somewhere," Justice said. "We need to find them."

"What are you people doing in here?" We all turned to find a big, burly guy standing in the doorway. "You can't be here. This area is restricted until further notice."

For a long moment, we all just stared at the guy. Then Molly, who was fierce but cute as a bug, gave him one of her trademark smiles. I counted down from ten to when the guy would melt into a gooey puddle near her dainty feet. Usually, I only got to eight. However, the security guy simply crossed his arms over a well-padded chest and glowered at her.

Molly took a step back as if she were so non-plussed by his non-reaction that she might fall over in a swoon.

"What are these clothes doing here?" I asked in my cop voice.

The man blinked. He hadn't expected that. "What? How should I know?"

I pulled my old badge out of my pocket and opened the card wallet to flash it. Yeah, I know. I was no longer a cop. Not the human kind anyway. But I'd taken to carrying the badge around with me just in case I needed an edge. "We're with the Community Safety Work Group. Mayor Desmond sent us to make sure this place was secure."

The man's expression softened slightly. "Oh," was all he said.

Stuffing the badge back into my pocket, I moved closer. I poked a finger hard into his squishy moobs and he took a step back, looking alarmed. "First of all, these things weren't here yesterday. Which means someone has been inside this stadium. That's not possible with the chains barring the entrances. Did you unlock a gate for someone?"

The big guy was in the hallway. His hands came up defensively. "No. I think those have been there..."

I poked at him again. "Secondly, why are *you* here? Nobody...I mean nobody...except this group should be in this stadium. It's considered a Level Ten disaster space. Level Ten," I repeated. "Do you know what that means?"

The guy took another step back and shook his head. He was starting to look a little pink around the gills.

"It means this place could come down around our ears at any moment. Who told you to be here?"

The guy glanced over his shoulder, toward a bright yellow door just past the snack area. "I...um..." He pointed toward the main gate. "I'll just go lock that back up."

"Take yourself out before you lock it."

He frowned. "But then, how will you all get out?"

I stiffened as if he'd insulted me beyond my ability to cope. I let fire light in my eyes and clenched my teeth until it gave me a headache. "Don't you worry about what we're doing..." I leaned closer and pointedly read the man's name tag... "Mr. *Fester*" I snarled his name out as if it was an affront to my sensibilities. "Now, get out of this structure!"

He turned around and ran toward the entrance end of the stadium, never looking back.

I cocked a gun with my hand and blew on a finger. "The bigger they are, the harder they fall."

Molly rolled her eyes. "Have you thought about the fact that he's going to see an intact chain when he reaches that entrance?"

"That's why we need to hurry. Come on." I took off running toward the yellow door. I had no idea what we would discover there, but I was definitely going to find out.

"I didn't know we had a Community Safety Work Group in Fort Wallace," Molly said to me. "And, I've lived here my whole life."

I shrugged, pulled my handgun, and reached for the knob. Glancing around at everybody, I said, "Ready?"

Juggler tugged Molly gently behind him and nodded.

Justice had his fancy, fan-shaped blades in his hands. I loved to watch him use those blades. It was like a ballet with blood. A dance with death. Grisly with grace. Too much?

"We don't know what's in there," Justice said. "Let's not attack first and ask questions later."

"If we wait too long, our brains might become monster food," Molly said. I noticed she was clutching the weapon she'd used at Peggy Sue's place, a long knife that, for her, was like a sword.

"You're thinking about zombies," I told her. "Ghouls only eat your innards."

"Not necessarily," Juggler said helpfully. "Sometimes they eat brains."

"Brains aren't their favorite though," Justice clarified.

Elvo barked as if adding his two cents to the conversation.

I stared at them. "Are you all done?"

They shrugged, looking at each other.

"Let's just agree that any of those body parts would be unpleasant to have ghouls chomp on, shall we?"

Mols rolled her eyes. "Let's go, Rae," she said in her "whatever" voice.

I wrapped my hand around the knob and pulled the

door open just enough to peer through. The space behind the door was empty and quiet. Light filled the room through the freshly opened door, illuminating all the corners and dissolving any shadows that might have been there.

I sniffed loudly, scenting musty air and old food, but no decomp.

So far, so good.

My weapon held in front of me in two hands, I slipped inside the room and looked around. There were boxes of straws and napkins and other concession-type things. A filthy window high on the outside wall allowed only dim threads of light to filter through and illuminate the space. Everything was covered in a thick layer of dust and the floor was moist near the base of the walls, as if something had been leaking for a long time.

Despite the feeling of disuse, there were marks in the dust coating the floor that told me the boxes had been shoved around fairly recently.

Justice pushed in behind me and stood frowning. "This is underwhelming."

"Was that Fester guy trying to distract us with this room?" Molly asked. She and Juggler stayed in the doorway. There really wasn't enough room for all of us to fit inside.

"It sure looks like it," I said. "But I don't know why he would."

A cool, damp breeze sifted over me and I jolted to a stop. "Where did that come from?"

"It smelled like the river," Justice said. "Doesn't one run past the back of this stadium?"

"The Maumee," Molly agreed. "But why would we be smelling it in here?"

"That's a good question," I said, moving to shove boxes

around. Another ribbon of cooler air, redolent with the stench of dead fish, wafted beneath my flaring nostrils. I shoved more boxes aside and turned to Justice as I came up against a rusted metal shelving unit. "Help me move this?"

With Juggler moving more boxes out of our way, we put our backs into moving the shelving unit. It didn't budge.

"Why is this thing so heavy?" I asked. I stepped back and wiped sweat off my brow with my dusty shirt.

"Maybe it's attached to the wall," Molly suggested.

We all looked at her and she shrugged. "My niece has toddlers and she bolts everything to the wall so they don't get flattened when they try to climb the furniture."

I gave her a look. "Flattened?"

She shrugged. "You know I'm not a kid person, Rae."

"Yeah. But that's cold even for you."

Molly shrugged. "Point taken."

And so was *her* point. I pulled out my cell and hit the flashlight, skimming the light over the shelving unit where it met the wall. Sure enough, one side was attached with three hinges. "Well, I'll be made into ghoul soup and served to the king."

"What did you find?" Molly asked, trying to shove past Juggler.

"This thing swings open," I told the group. I grabbed the unhinged edge and pulled, with Justice's help, until it was far enough away from the wall that we could slip through. Justice and I stepped through, stopping at the top of a set of rough-hewn stairs that disappeared into a black, unlit space at the bottom. My tiny phone light didn't do a thing to cut the blackness when I held it out in front of us. "Well, it looks as if we're going down," I finally said.

Elvo shoved his big head between us and growled.

Justice slid his gaze to me. "Elvo says..."

"I know what he said," I interrupted. "He said thar be ghouls down yonder."

"He didn't say it like Blackbeard the pirate. But, yep."

10

ALIGHARISTAMORGANISHLINKULA

Elvo pushed past us and bounced down the steps. I fought the urge to call him back, not knowing what we were going to bump up against at the bottom.

But he could take care of himself. Worst case, he could just incinerate the nasty things with Hell fire. Still, the big hound was like the rock you threw into a well to discover how deep it was. When he slipped into a darkness so complete it looked like he'd stepped off the edge of the world, I found it hard to completely fill my lungs.

"This passage tells me the ghouls have been here a while," Juggler said. "This wasn't just done in a few days."

Justice nodded. "The first inkling they'd managed to cross the dimensional border was nearly a month ago. But nobody could find evidence that they'd crossed, so the higher ups took a wait and see attitude."

"It seems they did too much waiting and not enough seeing," Molly snarked.

"I can't argue that now," Justice agreed. "Let's just hope

King Crunch hasn't dug himself in too deeply to extract. Like a tick."

I turned his way, a grin forming. "Now, I know that can't be his real name. It sounds like a breakfast cereal."

Juggler chuckled. "Nah. But his real name is too long to pronounce. It's just easier to go with a nickname. It's kind of endearing, don't you think? For such a fun-loving guy."

"What's his real name," Molly asked.

The silence was so long, I didn't think anybody was going to respond. But, finally, Justice said. "Aligharistamorganishlinkula."

"Say what?" Molly laughed.

"And that's just his first name," Justice said.

"Why so long?" I asked, shining my light on the steps below us.

"Ghouls take the names of their most powerful victims," he said. "It's like eating their victim's hearts. They view it as a statement of their dominance. But, instead of discarding the older names, they just keep adding on."

Up ahead, Elvo's deep growl turned to barking, and I knew he'd found our ghouls. "Look alive, people. We've got dead guys."

As we hit flat ground at the bottom, I heard water dripping from somewhere, and caught a whiff of rotted vegetation and dead fish. "I smell the river," I murmured.

Molly pointed to the far wall of the tunnel, where the mortar was dark and had a glossiness that told me water was probably leeching through the bricks.

We took off in a careful jog. Molly and I had our phone lights on and Justice and Juggler stayed inside that light and close to us. Ahead of us, flames illuminated what appeared to be an underground trail, which likely once belonged to some kind of subway system.

I'd known the city once had a system that fed the outskirts of Fort Wallace, but it had been defunct for longer than it had been in use. The city just hadn't been big enough to support it.

It seemed, however, that the king had found a use for the abandoned tunnel system, the walls of which were made of crumbling red brick rather than the roughly-hewn rock I'd been expecting.

Metal and wood supports spanned the arched ceiling, and an abandoned subway car sat between bent tracks that disappeared under fallen brick and other debris further down the tunnel.

Where the walls were intact, urban street art was rampant, and the abandoned car was nearly covered with paint of all colors. Bold, swirling artwork told a story of many people who'd made use of the tunnels, mostly homeless if I had to guess, and definitely living on the outskirts of humanity. I eyed the areas on either side of the abandoned car, wondering what secrets the shadows held there.

"Where's the hound?" Molly whispered, coming up next to me.

The cavern was silent. Nothing moved as our meager light flared over the space. Juggler and Justice stepped into the shadows on either side, weapons drawn. Molly stayed close to me, looking pale and tense as a disconcerting silence folded around us.

"It's too quiet," she told me, her whisper traveling through the enormous space like smoke.

I nodded. "Something's not right."

But despite our suspicions, nothing jumped out at us from the glooms. Elvo's snuffling grew softer as he moved along the broken rails of the old track in search of monsters. Juggler returned and pointed in the opposite direction.

"Molly and I will go that way. You and Justice follow Elvo. His scenting is better than ours. There's a good chance he's actually following something. Call us if you meet up with our ghoulish friends."

I nodded, looking up to find Justice just melting into the passage behind the big hound. The walls of the old trail were covered in soot-stained brick, the matte black surface eating the pitiful light my phone created. The ground was dusty and marked with decades of wandering footprints. Though the moldy scent of old death stained my nostrils, it never grew any stronger as we moved deeper into the impenetrable blackness of the tunnel.

"There's nothing here," I told Justice after several minutes. "If the ghouls had gone this way, they would have left a scent trail behind." I pointed to Elvo, who'd stopped ahead of us and was staring bleakly into the darkness, his tail tucked. "Even smoke breath is stumped."

Justice nodded, collapsing his magical fanned blades and sliding them into their hidden sheaths. "Elvo! We're leaving."

But the big hound stayed where he was, whining softly. I glanced at Justice and he suddenly had his blades in his hands again. Moving quickly forward, we eased up behind the Hellhound. "What is it?" I asked him softly. Crouching beside the big dog, I placed a hand on his shoulders and gave him a scratch.

He didn't so much as flap a back leg at the touch. He took another step forward and stopped, cocking his big head and whining again.

Justice and I shared a glance. Without words, we started forward. Justice moved across the passage and I kept to the path we'd been walking. Elvo fell into step with me, his whining getting louder with every step we took. The big hound seemed torn between worry and fear of whatever he sensed ahead.

The silence was so deep it became an entity unto itself, threatening and aggressive.

I found myself squinting into the blackness, desperate for a single sound to tell me what was there.

Justice lifted his blades, his big body on full alert.

My heart thudded anxiously in my chest, and my head throbbed with dread.

The phone light went out, leaving us in complete darkness.

A rumble began to build, the sound so low I thought at first I was imagining it.

Elvo pressed against my thigh, his big body vibrating with tension.

A gasp.

A thud.

A sharp, pain-filled cry.

Elvo flamed, sending ruby light into the darkness and I barely bit back a scream.

Ten feet away, a man lay across the rusted skeleton of the track, his clothing torn and bloody. His mouth opened and closed as if he were trying to speak, but the shallow wound beneath his chin likely made that painful.

Elvo's glowing gaze swung around the space, looking for the ghouls. There were none.

There was only the injured man who, I finally realized, wore the stadium security uniform.

I dropped to a knee next to him and quickly took inventory of his injuries.

His belly was torn and bloody, but, like the throat wound, the claw marks on his torso weren't deep. The ghouls didn't appear to have gotten to his insides. It was the same with his throat. The damage I could see was surface only. He was either very lucky...or...

I glanced up at Justice. "We need to get him out of here. I think this is a trap."

Justice sheathed his blades again and reached down for the man, lifting him into a fireman's carry and turning back the way we'd come.

Elvo turned and loped toward the main tunnel area where we'd come in. Footsteps thudded ahead of us and my heart sped. I transferred my gun to my right hand and yanked out a blade with my left.

A deep rumble started back behind us. "Is that a train?" I asked Justice as we broke into a run. He didn't respond, only picking up speed.

"Rae!" Molly screamed in front of us.

I jolted into a flat out run and Elvo shot past me. For a big dog, he was surprisingly fast.

A beat later, Molly screamed again. "Juggler!" Then the sound of flesh smacking into flesh and a wet grunt as Elvo snarled and tore at someone.

The rumble behind us had grown louder, and another rumble had started in front of us. When I pushed off a rusted track, the vibration of whatever was coming trembled through my foot. "I hope this isn't another sinkhole," I yelled.

Ahead of us, the red glow of Elvo's gaze spun and whirled, showing Juggler battling something and Elvo tearing into a wall of what had to be ghouls, though they were hard to get a fix on with all the motion.

Molly slashed at a bent, balding creature with glowing ruby eyes and claws for hands. She backed away as she fought it, trying to stay clear of the poisonous claws.

"Down!" I screamed and Molly flung herself sideways and down as I emptied my gun into the nasty creatures.

I tried to focus on the vulnerable areas, but with Juggler and Elvo thrashing around, it was safer to focus on the densest targets. Their mushy middles.

"Stairs!" I screamed at Molly, and for once she didn't argue. "Get him out of here!" I yelled at Justice.

He inclined his head. "I'll dump him and come back."

I didn't bother arguing because a second wall of shambling ghouls had emerged from the tunnel and into the faint light of the main cavern. Juggler and Elvo were still fighting as I slammed a fresh cartridge into my gun and started firing at the new wave of beasties.

We were outnumbered about a thousand to one. "Out Elvo! Juggler, we can't win. Let's retreat and regroup."

He didn't give any indication that he'd heard me, but he started backing toward the steps. I whistled and the Hellhound spun around, loping toward the stairs as I sprayed bullets around Juggler in the hopes of buying him some space.

Claws slashed at my back before I realized the things had reached me from the other tunnel. I was out of time. "Juggler!"

I turned and ran, firing bullets over my shoulder. When I hit the steps, I spun around and started slashing. Juggler was fighting his way toward me, when he got to me we went back-to-back, slashing and stabbing so fast our movements were a blur. Still the monsters kept coming. There were just too many. We wouldn't even make it up the stairs before we were overtaken. "Bounce!" Juggler yelled.

I nodded, though he wouldn't see me. He didn't need to tell me twice.

Thinking of my destination, I bounced.

11

I'M PROBABLY GONNA HAVE NIGHTMARES AFTER THIS

I landed in the middle of the ballfield and glanced around. Seeing Molly bending over the injured security guard a dozen yards away, I headed that way.

Juggler and Justice were nowhere to be seen.

"Where are they?" I asked my friend as she gazed at the face of her phone. She jumped slightly, looking up at me. "Sweet cherubs!" she exclaimed. "You scared the field dust out of me."

"Ha," I said in response. "Where's Justice?"

"Didn't you see him? He said he was going back down there."

"No. Dangit!" I started to pace around her. "We bounced out because there are too many of them." I scanned a look toward the stadium.

"What about Juggler?"

She blinked, looking around. "I have no idea. He was here a minute ago."

I bit back a curse and scraped my palms over my gritty face. It was like herding cats on Jupiter. I jerked my head toward the guard. "How is he? Did you call for an ambulance?"

"He hasn't woken up since Justice carried him up here. The 911 operator didn't think an ambulance would approach the stadium. Apparently, the entire area around this field is now considered unstable. They've set barriers several blocks out, surrounding us."

A low rumble that shook the ground beneath our feet emphasized her words.

"There are hundreds of ghouls beneath this stadium." A shudder rolled through me and I rubbed my arms. "There's nothing holding them beneath the ground." I knew we could bounce out of there if needed. But what about the humans in the area? My gaze focused on the pudgy face of the security guard. He had pale brown hair, cut short around his fleshy face, and thick eyelashes that fluttered as his eyeballs rolled beneath this lids. "He looks like he's having nightmares," I murmured.

"Can you blame him?" Mols asked.

I blinked, unaware that I'd spoken aloud. But I shook my head. "No. I'm probably gonna have nightmares after this too."

Molly nodded. Her phone rang and she looked down at the ID. "It's Rog. Should I answer it and tell him what we're doing?"

I snorted. "I dare you."

Her eyes sparkling, Molly answered the call, putting it on speaker. "Hey."

"Mollllsssss!"

She rolled her eyes. "Don't go all drama mama on me, Rog. I don't have time. Just tell me what's wrong."

"Don't have time?" he whined in his nasally voice. "Seriously? What could be more important than your Fall line?"

My bestie gave me an impish grin. "If you must know, we're fighting hordes of ghouls to save the city."

"Ghouls!" he screeched.

I snorted out a laugh and Molly's eyes twinkled. "Yeah. Stay inside and lock the doors. Whatever is going on at work, you're going to have to handle it. I'll call you when we get done here."

"Where's *here* exactly?"

I visualized Rog's eyes bulging like a frog's.

"At Wasp Stadium," Molly said.

"Mollllssssss!"

"Roger F. Bateman!" Molly barked out. "Calm down right this minute."

There was a moment of stunned silence. Then, the hysterical assistant said quietly, "That area has been condemned, Molly. The ground is falling away from beneath it. You. Will. Be. Killed."

Molly sighed. "I'm thinking the ghouls will probably kill us first."

A soft whining sound came through the line. "Get out of there," Roger tried again.

"I've got to go, Rog. Let's do lunch tomorrow. Or...maybe next week." She hung up as he started to scream at her again, cutting him off mid-shriek.

"Where am I?" a strangely high-pitched male voice asked. They turned to look at the security guard, who was trying to sit up and failing. His thick arms seemed to be made of rubber. I hurried over and helped him sit. He dropped his head into his hands and leaned forward. Dark sweat stains saturated the back of his pale blue shirt and formed deep arcs beneath his arms. The sour stench of fear and sweat wafted away from him. "What happened to me?"

"What do you remember?" I asked the man, crouching down beside him.

He shook his head, drying his face with a soggy sleeve. "I was doing my rounds at the end of my shift." He lifted his head and looked up at the sky. "Last night?" He looked at me. "What day is it?"

"Friday."

He blinked in shock. "Three days ago." A whimper emerged from his throat. "What happened to me?"

"Do you remember seeing anything else?"

"I went into the concession storage and..." He frowned. "Red eyes." He shook his head. "That can't be right. They... glowed."

Molly and I shared a look. Mine was filled with questions the guard likely would never answer. Questions such as, why was the man still alive? Why had the ghouls only given him surface injuries? Where had he been for three days? And where the heck were Elvo and the guys!?

First things first. We'd get the injured guard out of there and then find our team. "Can you walk?" I asked the man.

He fixed a dull look on me that didn't bode well for my intended task. "We need to get you to the gate so someone can take you to the hospital."

His eyes narrowed, something sharp sliding through his gaze. "I'm not leaving until I find out what's going on here." He shoved off the ground, the attempt to stand not in any way graceful or quick. But he managed it, straightening on legs that wobbled slightly. His brow glistened with sweat and he was panting from just that simple movement. "Come on," he told us. "I'm going back to that storage room."

"Wait," I said, easily catching up to his slow, lumbering steps. "You don't want to go in there again."

"Why not?" He frowned as the ground beneath our feet

rumbled and shifted. Ten yards away from us a hole opened up in the earth, dirt geysering up as the ground fell away. "The sinkholes." He brushed a shaky hand over his wet face and sighed. "I'd forgotten about those." He forced his shoulders back, pushing the rounded paunch of his belly out in the process. "I'll get you two to safety and then go." Changing direction, the guard waved us into motion. "There should be a cop car or two blocking the entrance to the stadium. They can unlock the gate and get you out." The guard turned to scour us with a questioning look. "What are you doing in here, anyway?"

I'll admit it. I was a little surprised his thoughts were sharp enough to wonder. Several possible lies flitted across my brain and I'd decided to tell him we were journalists trying to get the scoop on what was happening there, when Molly spoke up.

"Fashion show."

He frowned, ragged breaths heaving from his throat as he pushed onward. Fifty yards had never felt so far. "Fashion show? In the middle of an emergency?"

Molly sighed dramatically. "I know, I know. You sound like our boss. She told me to just leave the stuff here and she'd write it off on her taxes. But those dresses are some of my best work. I couldn't just let them get sucked into the ground like sequined worms."

He shook his head. "A few dresses aren't worth dying for," he said through panting breaths. Glancing at me, he added, "Are you in on this too?"

I threw up my hands. "Guilty as charged. Honestly, I don't care a whit about those dresses." I held up my hands as Molly gave me the expected glower. "Sorry, Mols. But I don't. I just wanted to make sure you got out of here alive."

The guard harrumphed. "Well, she will get out of here alive. But she's not going to save those dresses."

Molly gave an exaggerated sigh.

We finally walked beneath the concrete structure of the stadium, only twenty yards from the gated entranceway. The cool dimness felt divine after the broiling heat outside. The weather was ridiculously hot for early October. I tugged my sodden tee shirt away from my body and wished we could stay inside. But I suspected it was more dangerous beneath the half-moon shape of the stadium than out in the open. Out there, all we had to worry about was the ground falling out from under us. Inside, we might get killed by falling chunks of concrete as the structure turned brittle on unsteady supports. I eyed the walls and saw cracks that hadn't been there when we'd arrived, snaking through the concrete pillars that held up the seats.

Chunks of broken wall had already fallen to the floor and widening cracks snaked through the concrete floor.

The guard finally reached the gate. Putting two fingers into his mouth, he gave a couple of shrill whistles, then waved at the policemen pacing in front of their cars a block away. One of the cops said something into his radio and the other started jogging our way. I looked at Molly and she nodded. "I'm just going to run to the Ladies..."

The guard's eyes went round. "Have you lost your mind?"

But Mols was already running toward the restrooms, pretending she hadn't heard.

I rolled my eyes in faux commiseration. "Sorry. She has a nervous bladder. I'll go get her."

"No!" the guard yelled. "Stay. I'll go."

Like Molly, I ignored him, flinging a hand over my head and taking off at a run. By the time I reached the privacy wall for the Women's restroom, I could hear voices back by the gate. Then the clang of metal on metal.

"We need to skedaddle. They're unlocking the chain."

Molly didn't argue. We took off running, ducking past the ground-level seats and out of sight.

An argument rose from the direction of the gate and we ran faster, knowing our security guard was fighting against being escorted from the stadium. Good. He'd be safe and we'd be free to find our team. Speaking of which... "Didn't Juggler tell you where he was going?" I asked Molly.

She grimaced. "He said something. But, to tell you the truth I wasn't paying attention." She looked sheepish, but I laughed. "I wondered how you and Juggler got along so well. He's a bit much sometimes."

Molly shrugged. "He's actually very sweet. And, as you know, I can be a little tricky myself at times."

"Truth."

Molly poked me with her bony elbow. "You didn't have to agree so fast."

"True is true, Mols. Now give your big girl panties a tug and let's go find the guys. They're probably in a hot mess by now and are waiting for us to save them."

12

HE'S LIVING THE RUSE NOW

The storage room where we'd uncovered the door to the tunnels was empty. The door was open and the stench of ghoul was a living presence in the space. Molly and I stood at the top of the stairs and listened for any sounds that might tell us where the guys had gone.

Silence throbbed below.

"This isn't good," I whispered to Mols. "If they've gone back down there and there isn't the sound of a battle going on..."

"Then they've been overcome and the roaches have all scuttled back to the shadows," Molly finished for me, her pixie face filled with concern.

I thought about our options for a second, and then turned to her. "I need to go down there and see if I can find them. You need to stay here."

"Nope."

"Mols..."

"Don't even waste your breath trying to convince me to hide here like a sissy girl while you take on a thousand ghouls by yourself. It's not happening."

"There's no sense…"

"Nope."

"But…"

"Nopity, nope, nope."

I sighed, reaching for the big guns. "WWRD?"

She narrowed her gaze on me. "Huh?"

"What would Rog do?"

She scrunched up her face. "He'd hide under the bleachers like a wuss. What does that have to do with me?"

I snorted. "He would, wouldn't he?"

"Darn straight. I love that man and he's a great assistant, but he's been pretending to be a metrosexual male for too long. He's living the ruse now."

"Okay. Then here's what we're going to do…"

An explosion ignited nearby, shaking dust from the beams high above our heads. I sneezed violently and Molly ran to the single undersized window on the outside wall, peering out through the streaks of mud. "Oh, oh."

"Oh, oh?" I asked, hurrying over to squeeze in beside her. "I don't want to hear that right now, Mols. We've got enough on our plates at the moment."

But whether I wanted more problems, or not, I had them. The area near the back gate was a smoking cloud of dust and concrete chunks, dust still shooting from its depths.

Sirens blared in the distance and lights flashed as emergency crews no doubt thundered our way. Molly reached out and clamped a claw-like hand onto my wrist. "We need help, Rae. There are too many of those things and, at the rate the stadium is going under, there's going to be nothing left to save by the time we find the guys."

If there was anything left now, I thought glumly. The thought made my pulse skyrocket and yanked air from my lungs. I fought the need to double over, holding my suddenly roiling stomach. Instead, I focused on breathing in and out.

As I straightened up, I heard a sound that had me whipping around. A shadow moved through the door. A shadow with glowing red eyes and gleaming white fangs.

My tension eased down a few notches.

"Thank the goddess," I said, wrapping my arms around Elvo's thick, furry neck. "You're okay."

The big dog chuffed indignantly, no doubt annoyed that I'd think otherwise, and licked my hair. I was so happy to see him that I didn't even yell at him for coating me in dog slobber. "Where are Justice and Juggler?" I asked the big hound. "Are they with you?"

I peered hopefully through the door into the concession area across the walkway, hoping to see the two men following. There were no large males striding our way. My short-lived relief spiked back into fear. "Where are they?"

Elvo made a woo woo noise and spun around, disappearing back through the door.

"I think he wants us to follow him," Molly said.

Biting back a snide response, I started after him. If Elvo had come to show us where Justice and Juggler were, that meant they were in trouble.

The kind of trouble they couldn't get out of themselves.

We didn't get far before there was another explosion, the second one much closer. The concrete floor in front of us exploded upward in jagged chunks that slammed into the concession counters, collapsing large sections of them. We ducked into the nearby Ladies' restroom, but I was still clocked on the head by a sizeable piece of debris. I fell sideways and bumped into Molly, taking us both to the ground.

Molly's head slammed into the floor and I mentally cursed myself for not being more careful.

Warm liquid ran from my hairline and dripped onto the floor as I tried to sit up. Unfortunately, as soon as I managed it the world went wonky, swimming around me like a bad acid trip.

Elvo paced around us, his claws clicking like a metronome on the tile floor. He bumped me with his wet nose, whining softly. "I'm okay, buddy," I said as pain sliced through my skull. "It's just a bump from the sky falling on my head." I moved slowly, turning to get a look at Molly. To my relief, her eyes were open and she was staring at me. "You alive?"

She held up a finger. "Give me a minute. I'm checking all my systems now."

I gave her a grin. If she was being witty, she was okay. Pushing to my feet, I offered her my hand. "Unfortunately, we don't have a minute. We're running out of real estate here. We need to find the guys and skedaddle."

The sirens and shouting from the street beyond the fence had gone silent. I could only assume that the rescue force was taking a cautious profile, assessing their options before coming inside. Which made sense considering that they thought the stadium had been evacuated.

"Okay," Mols said, "Where are we going now?" She grimaced. "Please tell me we're not going back down into that cavern."

Avoiding her gaze, I said, "Um..."

A high, shrill scream jerked my attention toward the gate. Several more just like it pierced the air and yanked my pulse into overdrive.

"That sounded bad," Molly said, wiping a thin trail of blood off her face with a sleeve.

Yeah. It did. "I hope that's not the security guard we just saved?"

"We have to check, Rae."

Expelling a gust of frustrated air, I scrubbed a hand over my face. "Let's go."

We ran. The screams had died down by the time we took off, which was likely a bad sign. As we approached the gate, I slowed, taking in the scene. An ambulance was parked haphazardly at the curb, the back door hanging open and the vehicle empty. A stethoscope lay on the street, forgotten.

One police cruiser still blocked the entrance to the stadium. The others were gone. I saw no cops inside or outside the vehicles. A block away, a firetruck sat with lights still flaring. Nobody moved around the truck, but I could make out two heads behind the glass. They weren't moving.

"Where is everybody?" I murmured.

Though the question had been rhetorical, Molly shrugged.

The gate chain was still in place, and there was no sign of our security guard. His badge lay in front of the gate, looking as if someone had trampled it. But he was gone. Had he taken a turn for the worse? Maybe he'd been more injured than I'd thought. Had someone taken the body away?

"Where's the guard?" Molly asked, looking confused.

"I don't know," I said, my voice quiet. "But I hope that wasn't him." I pointed to a red puddle on the concrete beyond the gate.

Molly's eyes went wide. "Do you think somebody attacked him?"

That was what it had sounded like to me. Then I spotted two feet in heavy black boots sticking out from beneath a large evergreen nearby. I couldn't see much beyond the dark blue cuff of what looked like uniform pants. Grimacing, I said, "Stay here, Mols. I'm going to go check that out."

She nodded, her bottom lip firmly clamped between her teeth. "Be careful, Rae. Something feels...off about this."

She wasn't wrong. Warning bells were clanging in my brain and my heart was pounding. "I'll be fast. I'm just gonna bounce over there, check his pulse and then bounce back."

Molly didn't argue, but she was hugging herself.

I let my mind picture the spot where I needed to go and waited. The ground didn't shift beneath my feet. My body didn't disapparate and reform near the tree.

"Rae?"

I frowned. Then tried again. Nothing. "Mols, I can't bounce."

Her expression, which had been plenty worried before, turned panicky. "But you bounced earlier."

"Yeah," I responded in a slightly dazed tone. But only within the fence line."

"What's going on, Rae?"

I wished I knew. "Maybe the king put a spell on the stadium grounds that keeps anyone from moving magically into or out of it." If he had, it had happened since we'd first arrived because we'd bounced into the stadium. Which, when I thought about it, was probably why he'd decided to create the containment spell. "Whatever's happening, it's clear we can't bounce out."

Another explosion sent dirt and rocks skyward. That one had been in the outfield, the debris crashing into the grassy hill where families with small children always watched the Wasps for free, spreading blankets and picnics for toddlers who couldn't sit still.

Chunks of rock slammed into the vibrant carpet of

green, ripping pieces out of it and battering the fencing behind the hill.

"Who's doing this?" Molly asked, sounding angry. I knew my bestie too well to believe it was just anger, though I was sure that was part of it. She was scared. And anger was less debilitating than giving in to the fear.

The obvious answer was the ghoul king. But I had no idea why he'd draw so much attention to the spot he'd claimed for his nest.

I pulled her into a quick hug. "Let's go find the guys and get out of here."

Her hazel gaze haunted, Molly rubbed her hands over her face and nodded her agreement.

In the distance, the haunting sound of a canine howling had Molly and me exchanging looks. I hadn't noticed when Elvo left us, and had no idea where he'd gone. But it sounded as if he was on the other side of the stadium. "This way," I said, and we took off running again.

Our feet hit the cracked concrete of the stadium but didn't slow. The last place I wanted to be was inside that building if another explosion rocked its foundation.

We ran straight through, the sunlight hitting our faces like a slap as we emerged from the dimly lit stadium and past the seats.

"Hey!" someone yelled. We slowed and looked around. A woman was heading our way, her slender form attractively draped in a flower-covered cotton dress. The dress had short, fluttery sleeves and narrowed at her slender waist, flaring slightly as it draped past her knees. She had long, blonde hair that fell in soft curls around her shoulders and danced around her breasts as she hurried toward us. "Hi," she said, smiling. "I'm looking for my husband. Have you seen him?"

A sense of strangeness slipped over me. A Twilight Zone moment, fraught with weirdness. The woman slowed to a stop a few feet away, her wide smile showing perfect, white teeth. "Have you seen him? He's a security guard here."

Dread slipped through me and Molly and I shared a look.

"Can you describe him for us?" I asked, trying to keep my tone pleasant.

She described our "disappeared" guard. "We did see him a while ago. But I think he left." I didn't want to tell the woman he was dead until I knew for sure that he was. "Do you mind my asking how you got in here? The place is on lockdown."

She laughed prettily, tossing her hair so that the sunlight glistened off the shiny strands, turning it to spun gold. "Don't tell anybody this, but there's a section of fence back there that's ripped open. Daniel and I sneak through there all the time and come watch the stars at night. When the lights are off, this is the best place in the city to see the stars."

"Daniel's your husband?" Molly asked.

The woman nodded, smiling. "He's such a romantic, my Danny."

"I'll bet," I said. "You know it's not safe to be here, right?" I swung an arm around the area to direct her attention to the torn-up ground and the badly damaged stadium.

She nodded. "That's why I came. Danny takes his job way too seriously. He'd stay here until the whole place sinks into the ground if I didn't make him come home."

I thought of those boots sticking out from under the tree and my heart twisted with pain for the woman. But Danny apparently wasn't the only one in his family to make bad safety choices. "You need to get out of here. Go back through the broken fence. If we see your husband, we'll send him home."

"Really? You'd do that for me?" Her smile was too bright. Her gaze just short of simple.

"We would. We will."

"Okay." She started to turn away and stopped. "Oh. By the way."

I never even saw the attack coming. One second I was rolling my eyes over the woman behind her back. And the next, she was flying toward me, snarling like a feral beast. She hit my chest and wrapped herself around my torso like a giant spider. I looked into glassy blue eyes and saw nothing behind them. Where had the sweet but not-too-bright housewife gone? The conformation was too stark. For a few beats, I had trouble wrapping my mind around it.

But there were square, blunt teeth clacking near my throat, and coral-pink claws digging into my shoulders.

"Rae!" Molly appeared behind my attacker, her blade in her hand, but unsure what to do with it. "Should I stab her?"

A slender leg wrapped around my thighs and squeezed so tight I screamed with pain. The woman looked like she weighed a hundred-and ten-pounds max, but she had the strength of a cyborg. With my attention temporarily split, she took advantage and pushed off the ground with her free leg, yanking my balance out from under me. I went down, slamming hard into the dirt with the housewife still riding my front.

"Rae!?"

I didn't know what to tell Molly. The woman didn't appear to be a ghoul. But she was definitely several fruit loops short of a bowl. "Just give me a minute..." I threw my weight sideways and pushed off with one foot, succeeding in pinning her beneath me. Unfortunately, my weight brought me closer to those clacking teeth, and warm blood ran down my arms from the clutching pink claws.

I punched the woman in the face and she barely reacted. Froth bubbled from her pale pink lips, splattering onto her flowered dress when she jerked her head and snapped, trying to tear my flesh. Then she smiled and it was the most horrible thing I'd ever seen.

"Maybe you should..."

Molly was suddenly there, her pale hand clutching something angular and gray. It wasn't a knife. But it was effective. My bestie held the rock over her head in both hands and slammed it down, giving a feral yell as the rock crashed into the woman's skull.

With a soft whoosh of air, the housewife went limp, her eyes fluttering closed.

I shoved off her and scooted away, panting. "Nice work, partner."

Molly was panting too, no doubt from stress. She threw the rock away with a grimace. "What just happened, Rae?"

"I have no idea. She wasn't a ghoul. Drugs, maybe? You've heard of that zombie drug that makes people crazy strong and impervious to pain?"

Molly nodded. "Okay then. I wonder if she was telling the truth about the hole in the fence?"

"I stood up, glancing around. "She came from back there, I think. I can see an equipment building. Let's see if we can get some rope to tie her up with and then we can go find the guys."

"Sounds like a plan."

The shed was tucked into a back corner of the property, beneath an oversized evergreen that, appeared to have been pooping pine needles and pinecones onto the grass surrounding it for years. Our feet crunched over the pinecones and smashed the brown needles, the scent of pine rising up around us. The door to the metal building was padlocked. It took me only a few minutes and a rock to break it open. The big door rolled back with a sharp creak. The smell of engine oil and gasoline replaced the more pleasant scent of pine. A mid-sized tractor with a mower attachment took up most of the space. A drag hung from one wall, an assortment of other maintenance tools around it. We carefully picked our way around the tractor, looking for rope. I headed for the wall with the drag and other tools, figuring that would be the most likely spot to hold a coil of rope.

But I saw no rope.

"Um, Rae?"

I lifted the drag away from the wall and looked at the floor where it had pooled. There was a small toolbox with a hammer and some screw drivers, but no rope.

"Rae!?"

I answered without turning. "Huh?"

"You need to see this." Molly was staring down at the ground near the mower attachment, a frown marring her features.

"Did you find rope?"

"Yeah. But..."

I picked my way around the tractor and looked down. There were several pieces of rope there. But they had already been cut, the pieces painted with blood. "That's not good."

"Who do you suppose was being held here?" Mols asked. "Clearly against their will."

I sighed, a sharp sense of dread skimming through me. "That's a very good question."

13

HELLO NIGHTMARE

"Woof!"

"Elvo!" I stepped back out into the sun and saw the big hound standing beneath the evergreen tree in the shade, a pinecone clutched between his hairy jaws. I brushed a clump of dirt off his glossy black coat. "Where'd you go? I thought you were going to help us find the guys."

"Woof!" His thick fan of a tail whipped the air as his large white teeth crunched down on the pinecone. He whipped around and trotted toward the spot where we'd left the woman.

When we got there, she was gone.

"That woman has a skull of steel," I told Mols.

"No joke. Should we go looking for her?"

I wasn't exactly excited about doing the giant spider dance with the goofy housewife again. "I don't want to waste the time. I'm sure *she'll* find *us*." Unfortunately. "We need to find Justice and Juggler." I walked over and tugged the soggy, flattened pinecone from Elvo's big maw. Long slobber strings followed the thing out with my fingers. "Ugh! Gross."

Elvo bounced around, tail wagging.

"No messin' around now," I told the Hellhound mutt. "Show us where Justice and Juggler are."

"Woof!" He spun around and jogged away, toward the stadium. He entered the dugout area and trotted past the player benches, ducking into a door marked, "Locker Rooms."

There were two doors, one for Home and one for Visitor. I pushed the first door open and was assailed by the scents of stale sweat, dirty socks, and floor cleanser. After doing a quick search of the stalls, I followed Molly to the showers.

She stood in the center of the space, her back to me and her form rigid. Her gaze was locked onto a slender form folded onto the floor in the center of a shower stall. A form wearing a flowery dress.

Molly looked up as I stopped next to her. "I found the happy housewife."

"You did." The woman's eyes were closed and blood congealed in her hair. She didn't appear to be breathing. "Mols..."

"I killed her, Rae. I just took that rock and bashed her in the head and now she's dead."

"We don't know that's what killed her," I said.

Molly gave me a flat look, clearly irritated by my trying to comfort her. She'd always been an A++ personality. Hard working, single-minded to the point of psychosis, and brutally honest with herself when she didn't live up to her own expectations. And her expectations for herself far exceeded her expectations of others.

I was the one who'd traipsed through life looking for good enough rather than perfect. My way rarely gave me angst. Rarely. But the first life I'd taken as an experienced street cop still lived with me. I still woke occasionally in a regret-filled sweat from nightmares of that "kill or be killed" moment.

To say that I knew exactly how she felt would be an understatement.

But Molly wasn't ready to hear me tell her it would be all right. She might never be.

I crouched down beside the woman and placed my fingertips at the pulse-point in her throat. Her skin was cool to the touch. Her flat-ish chest didn't rise.

"She's dead, isn't she?"

I started to rise. To tell Molly the woman was indeed gone. When a set of fingers with familiar pink fingernails that were honed to deadly points wrapped around my wrist. I tensed for an attack, trying to yank my hand away, and found myself trapped by a strength the woman shouldn't have had. She yanked me down to her level, her lips so close to my ear that whisps of cool air from her words tickled my skin. "Stop...them..."

She fell back to the ground and released air in a soft rush.

"What did she say?" Molly moved into my space, her eyes wide with shock. "Rae!?"

I stumbled backward, taking Molly with me. I wasn't sure if the woman was dead or alive. "She said, stop them." I wrapped an arm around Molly, suddenly feeling as if we'd fallen past *Twilight Zone* to something even weirder. Maybe a *Stranger Things* remake.

Elvo bumped my leg with his big head, yanking me from a dazed fog. He turned around and loped toward a scarred wooden door in a back corner of the room. Snuffling around beneath the door, he stood expectantly until I opened it. Then he took off down another set of stairs, which I feared would lead us back to the ghoul-filled cavern. Sighing with resignation, I pulled my weapons and took a deep breath to center myself, releasing it slowly.

Behind me, Molly held her short sword in one hand and had the other hand on my shoulder as we descended together.

Elvo didn't seem tense, although the stairwell we were descending seemed to go much deeper than the one leading from the storeroom. Was it possible we weren't going to the same subterranean cavern as before?

The first thing I became aware of was the icy air, which felt cold enough to refrigerate meat. I also noticed a soft light flickering at the bottom of the steps, which were built of wood, clearly added recently, as opposed to the rock-hewn ones we'd descended before. The illumination flickered from a sconce hanging on the wall near the steps. Somewhere in the distance, water fell in a constant trickle that was likely the cause of the damp feel and musty smell of the place.

Elvo took off and immediately disappeared into the darkness. I grabbed the sconce, lit by some kind of oil-drenched rag, and hurried to catch up. Molly's light footsteps followed mine, so close she kept stepping on the back of my shoes.

The third time she did it I jolted to a stop and rounded on her.

She threw up her hands, palms out. "I know! Sorry. I just don't want to get separated in this place. It's terrifying down here."

She wasn't wrong about that. Where the cavern with the old subway train had given off a sad, forgotten air, the dark, moldy passage we currently walked just felt like a giant grave.

It even smelled like a grave.

I shuddered beneath the thought and reached back for Molly's hand. "Come up here with me. I need a binkie."

A low growl vibrated on the air. My head whipped around to find Elvo staring at me, a full set of large white teeth exposed as he growled in my direction.

"Oh, oh." I held up my hands. "Hey, buddy. We're friends, right?"

He snarled and I stepped sideways, my hand reluctantly falling to the hilt of my knife.

But Elvo's gaze didn't shift with me. It was still fixed on the spot where I'd stood.

Or the spot behind where I'd been standing. The very empty spot. *No, no, no, no, no!*

Molly!

"Where?" I asked diving toward that spot and dropping to my knees. I dug frantically in the dirt, looking for some kind of trapdoor or something. "Where'd she go, buddy?" I asked Elvo as he pressed up against me, his tail down and his throat still rumbling. "Did you see what took her?" Tears burned my eyes and a wave of pure panic swept me, making it hard to breathe. If I lost Molly after yelling at her because she was sticking too close... Swallowing a scream, I barely managed to draw air into my lungs.

Elvo whined, the sound pitiful.

I jumped up and looked around, seeing no nooks or crannies where someone could be hiding. I even looked up to the top of the cavern, the jagged surface flat and black with shadows. It was possible she could be there. The shadows might have hidden her, but I doubted it. They weren't that thick.

She'd just disappeared into thin air. Just like Juggler. Like Justice.

I swiped angrily at tears, silently scolding myself for

being weak when I needed to be strong. I stood there for a minute, trying to figure out what to do next. I'd set out to find Justice and Juggler and had only managed to lose Molly.

Sweet cherubs on a new blue moon. Had I fallen down a rabbit hole? The world had turned upside down and inside out and I wasn't sure where I was in the resulting tangle.

"Woof!"

"Not yet," I told Elvo. I was reluctant to leave the spot where I'd last seen Molly. It felt too much like leaving her behind. But if I found the guys, they could help me find Molly. So, after several more minutes of searching, I gave up. "Okay," I told him. "Let's find Justice. Maybe he'll know where she was taken."

Elvo took off at a jog, heading into a part of the passage that seemed even darker than the rest.

Awesome.

"Maybe you could find a more terrifying place to search," I groused. Fortunately for him, Elvo seemed impervious to my grumping. He didn't respond. He just stepped into the deeper shadows and...disappeared.

I panicked. "No!" Without thinking, I took off running. I didn't think about whether I could be walking into a trap, or at the very least, a dangerous situation. I was determined that I wasn't going to be left all by myself in that stupid, sinking stadium.

But there was no sight of the hound.

He'd just disappeared.

Like all the others.

I threw back my head and howled my frustration into the moldy darkness. Screaming until my throat was raw. Then I collapsed to my knees in the dirt, fighting not to hyperventilate.

"Are you all right?" an unfamiliar male voice asked.

I jerked in surprise. Jumping to my feet and whipping around with my blade in my hand.

A young man stood several feet behind me. He was wearing charcoal slacks, a perfectly ironed white button up shirt, and shiny black dress shoes. His red-blond hair was neatly combed with a side part, giving him a slightly geekish look that was only exacerbated by the square tortoiseshell glasses that did nothing to hide his ebony eyes. He spared my weapon a quick, disinterested glance, favoring me with a sweet smile.

"Who are you?" I kept my distance, the memory of the crazy housewife still fresh in my mind.

"Call me Henri," he said, the smile widening.

"Okay, Henri," I said, nodding. "What are you doing down here in this disgusting place?"

He looked startled. Glancing around, he lifted his arms. "You don't like dark, dank places?"

I gave him a flat look, thinking he was joking. But his expression gave me pause. The guy's dark gaze sparkled as he looked around the cavern. He really did look like he loved it.

Henri sighed. "This place reminds me of my childhood playroom. I used to hide from my nurse by climbing the walls and clinging to the stalactites." He laughed gaily. "She used to get so angry."

The creep factor of the whole thing was getting to be more than I could handle. I'd had more weirdness than I could take. "Okay, Henri. I don't know who you are and I don't really care." Actually, I had my suspicions. "I just want my people back and we'll be on our way."

"Your people? Ah. Yes. The two men and the girl." He

nodded. "They promise to be such grand additions to my court."

My stomach twisted with alarm and I closed my eyes for a beat. When I opened them again, I lost my composure. "Where are they, you sick pile of worm poop." Lifting my gun, I stepped toward him. At that point, it wouldn't take much for me to spray him with a wall of bullets.

Henri, the ghoul king, looked at my weapon and shook his head. With a flick of his fingers, the weapon began spewing out the slimy, wriggling bodies of dozens of worms. Despite myself, I gave a little yelp and dropped the weapon. I mentally berated myself for being such a wussy girl. I'd always hated worms. As a kid, when my dad had taken me fishing, I'd refused to use live bait because I'd hated the feel of them writhing against my fingers.

A soft rustling sound warned me that we were no longer alone. I lifted my gaze and glanced toward the shadows. Which had begun to writhe and wriggle like the worms. A crowd of nasty, drooling ghouls in ragged, mud-coated clothing moved out of the glooms and swayed in my direction.

Hello, nightmare.

14

EW. THAT'S NASTY

Dread a sour taste in my mouth, I stared at Henri for a beat, before asking. "Why are your people so repulsive and you're..."

"Gorgeous?"

I didn't want to feed his delusions about himself, so I snorted. "Human looking."

The crowd of ghouls shifted constantly, not moving forward so much as just...moving. They shifted from side to side, their feral red gazes a disorienting glow that forced me to keep one eye on them at all times.

"What exactly are we working toward here?" I asked Henri, my hands tightening on my weapons. The single blade and the gun with limited bullets, weren't nearly enough to take out hundreds of ghouls.

"I don't know what *you're* working toward, my dear," the king said smoothly. "But *I'm* building out my kingdom."

"Why come here to do that?" I asked, as much to keep him talking as out of real curiosity.

He shrugged, lifting his arms and looking around. "You have to ask? This dimension has such lovely underground spaces. And such wonderful resources for fresh...flesh." He grinned as if he'd made a great joke.

I curled my lip. "You don't belong here. You need to go back where you came from."

He laughed. "That's not going to happen."

"Then you and I are going to have a problem."

"And what, exactly, do you plan on doing about it?" he asked.

I had no idea. At the moment it was me against a ghoulish world. And those weren't odds favoring a successful conclusion.

Right on cue, the shadows to my side split and I jumped to view what fresh Hell was coming my way. I was surprised to see Elvo trotting toward me with something between his jaws.

Henri hissed and I spun back toward him, lifting my blade. The perception of the ghoul king looking human disappeared when I looked at the disjointed jaw, spread wide enough to clamp down on somebody's head, and the long black tongue wagging in the air.

"Ew," I said, taking another step back. "That's nasty, Henri."

He lifted hands that had black claws instead of nails and hissed again.

He really didn't like the Hellhound.

There had to be a good reason for that.

Elvo stopped near my feet and dropped one of Justice's fan-shaped blades in the dirt.

Proof that he'd found them?

It had to be. I clasped the big dog's silky black ruff, the thick fur better than a handle as I scooped up Justice's blade and we started to back away. The wall of ghouls shifted forward, a low moan filling the underground passage and throbbing against my ears.

In response, Elvo took a step closer to them and shook himself, fire rolling over his enormous form. Flames danced in his usually kind brown eyes. Fire licked off the end of this tail. And flame dipped like melted wax off his big, floppy ears.

The ghouls swayed harder, their leathery faces stuck in a rictus of death and decay.

Henri hissed again, but when I turned around he was gone.

In fact, they'd *all* disappeared.

I fell to my knees and wrapped my arms around Elvo, burying my face in his fur. "I've never been happier to see anyone," I told him. "I could use a few more like you right now."

"Woowoo!" Elvo said with excitement.

I stood wearily. "Now, will you please stop messing around and show me where Justice and Molly are?"

He took off again, leading me out of the underground nightmare, back into the sunshine, and across the torn and broken field. The big dog effortlessly loped up the many stairs leading to the top of the stadium. When we reached the top, I turned and looked out over the wreckage of Wasp Field.

It looked like the site of a bombing.

The well-groomed field was pocked with dips, the grass torn and chunks of wood and metal from the surrounding structures littering its surface. From the spot where I stood, I could just make out the equipment shed and imagine the torn fencing behind it. Why hadn't the ghouls left through that breach? Or had they? Surely they didn't think they could lay claim to the stadium forever. At some point, human first responders would make it into the place and do what was needed to restore it to its former glory.

Or would they? I remembered the screams of the apparently dead security guard. Were the police compromised? Had they killed him?

Aside from that concern, geological changes below the earth's crust might not be something that could be overcome. The stadium might be shuttered and closed forever. If that happened, the ghoul king...Henri...would have the hidey hole he clearly wanted to create his monsters. And Fort Wallace would be sitting on a powder keg of future trouble.

"Woof!"

I glanced up to find Elvo standing beside the door to the press box. He was a magical canine, able to scare off hundreds of slavering ghouls with a single fiery look. But he couldn't turn the handle of a door. After all, he had no opposable thumbs.

"Coming, buddy," I said. "Just admiring the view." I ran up the remaining flights of stairs and reached for the door. To my surprise, it opened easily. I followed Elvo inside, my hands clutching my weapons and my heart pounding. I stepped through the door and stopped, my gaze sliding over what appeared to be a much larger space than I'd expected. The front part consisted of a long counter with a line of rolling chairs pushed beneath it. Microphones lined the counter, and a variety of other electronic equipment hung above and behind the counter. Large sliding glass doors could be pulled across that area to sever it from the rest of what looked like a fairly upscale apartment.

Behind the press box was a large living area, with plush couches arranged around a massive television hanging on the wall. The back wall was all glass, giving

whoever lounged in that room a beautiful view of downtown Fort Wallace, the view anchored by the downtown
square.

What the apartment didn't have were my friends. "Um,
Elvo?"

He walked over to a door at the side of the room and
shoved it with his wide nose. It had been open a few inches
and the door slid silently wider when he pushed it. A pile of
laundry lay mounded up in front of what appeared to be an
oversized shower stall.

Strange to have a shower stall in the press room. But,
okay. Somebody liked the creature comforts. I moved inside
the room and looked around, seeing what I presumed was a
closet door on the side wall.

I pulled it open.

The door led to a small, but well-furnished bedroom
whose outer windows looked out over the city, just as they
had in the living room. But there was a slight difference.
Justice was on the other side of the window glass, shuffling
along a narrow ledge with his eyes closed.

"Ah!" I ran to the nearest window that opened and
quickly unlocked it, yanking it open and sticking my upper
body outside. "Justice, what are you doing?"

To my horror, he appeared to be sleep walking. It was a
miracle he hadn't fallen off the ledge yet. And if he fell
where he was, unforgiving concrete waited for him three
floors below. "Justice! You need to wake up."

He ambled onward, the ledge not even wide enough for
one of his big feet. All it would take would be one slight
misstep...one unbalanced moment.

"Rae?" I whipped around at the sound of Molly's voice.
She was standing inside a closet, blinking rapidly. "Where
are we?"

I held up a finger. "Thank the goddess you're okay. Hold that thought. I need to..."

A pigeon flew smack into Justice's face and squawked, wings flapping wildly as it tried to reverse flight away from him. My guide stopped for a beat and then took another step forward, eyes still closed.

A hawk dove at the pigeon.

The birds erupted into a spray of feathers and slashing beaks and Justice seemed oblivious to it all. He took another step and was slashed across the cheek by the frantic pigeon as it tried to find an escape between him and the hawk.

Justice jolted to a stop, frowned, and his eyes slowly opened. He blinked, looked at the birds, and then slowly turned toward me. "Rae? Why are you on a ledge?"

"Try again, buddy." Something soft plopped by my feet and I looked down to find a bed pillow with moist fang marks in its dented middle. "Thanks, fire-breath." I stuck my head back outside. "Lean into the windows and hide your face," I warned my partner. "I'm going to shoo these guys away."

He just blinked at me, still looking confused.

I swung the pillow at the hawk, earning myself, or really my pillow, a few slashes from the angry predator. "Get lost, mean and ugly. You're crampin' my rescue style." After I swung at it a few more times, the big hawk lifted away with an angry screech and left.

Rather than moving his act to a kinder gentler part of town, the stupid pigeon landed on the ledge in front of my partner, and commenced to bobbing its fool head and pecking at the windows.

"Rae...I don't feel..."

I glanced up just in time to see Justice crumple and start to fall. "Elvo!"

I grabbed for Justice, managing to snag the waist of his jeans as he toppled sideways.

Somehow, Elvo snatched his ankle and we just barely kept him from falling. But I couldn't lift my partner through the window. He was too heavy. Elvo could probably do it if I got out of the way, but I was struggling with the idea of letting go.

Elvo growled around Justice's soggy pant leg.

"I know. But I'm terrified to release him."

"Here," Molly's still drowsy voice said. I turned to find her holding a long piece of fuzzy fabric toward me.

"What's that?"

"A robe tie. Loop it under his arms and then you'll have the leverage to pull him inside."

"Oh. Yeah. That might work. I grinned. "Thanks, Mols."

"Grrrrr!"

"Right. Stay on task, Rae," I scolded myself. Throwing one end of the tie over his back and then fighting to pull it around him without letting go, I almost lost my grip on Justice several times. A few minutes of sweaty struggles later, I had him. Taking a deep breath and releasing it, I quickly released his waistband and wrapped the tie around my hands. "Now, Elvo!"

He yanked, I yanked, and Justice spilled into the room, landing on his head and knees. Not pretty, but effective.

I turned to my bestie. "Leave it to you to save the day with a fashion accessory." I narrowed my gaze. "Are you okay? You guys look a little wonky."

She shook her head. "I don't remember how I got here. And my shoulder hurts." She rubbed a spot high on her left shoulder. Her fingers came away stained with blood.

"You've been cut." I tugged her shirt aside and barely kept from swearing. "The cuts aren't deep." I tipped her chin up and looked into her hazel eyes. They looked normal, if a little foggy. But...there. Did something just slide through them?

I dropped to my knees next to Justice and found cuts on his shoulder too. Dread and pain swamped me, taking the starch out of my spine. I all but fell backward against the bed.

It couldn't be.

My gaze lifted to Elvo's. I saw the knowledge in his liquid brown gaze too. His silky tail swept the carpet under him in hesitant strokes.

Tears burned my eyes. My friends had been marked by the ghoul king. Did that mean they were going to turn into ghouls?

Or maybe they already had.

15

TAKE MY EX. PLEASE

A soft thump lifted all three of our gazes toward the ceiling. "What's up there?" I asked Justice and Molly.

She gave me a flat look, crossing her arms over her chest. "Why do you think I would know that?"

I gave her one right back. "Because up until a few minutes ago, you were at one with the closet. I figured maybe you were exploring in there."

She shook her head. Her knees seemed to give out on her and she dropped to the bed. She looked frighteningly pale.

Justice rolled to his feet and wavered in a crouch. At first, I thought he was making a combat readiness statement, but looking back, I just think he was considering yarking. "I don't remember how we got here."

"Okay." I always loved it when a man answered a different question than he was asked. Our history books always put men in the hunter-gatherer class. But the truth was that they mostly only gathered word salad. And then flung it around like monkeys flinging feces.

Take my ex. Please. Tom would have made a consum-
mate politician. He never answered a direct question. Never
really gave out any useful information, but he always sent
words out into the universe like flocks of geese. Or a murder
of crows. Not really caring if the words matched the question. The world could do with them as they would.

"I think it's safe to assume the ghouls immobilized you
somehow. But the real question is why are you *here*?" It was
a rhetorical question. I didn't expect an answer.

Walking over to the closet, I flipped on the light. There,
high above my head was a small rectangle of ceiling that
was offset inside an opening by a couple of inches. An attic
space. Judging by the thumping, someone was up there.

Whoever it was, they hadn't done a good job of setting
their hidey hole to rights after climbing up there. I lifted the
hanging bar out of its supports and dumped a bunch of
empty hangers to the floor. Then I used the pole to poke the
loosened rectangle of ceiling and shove it upward. "Who's
up there?"

Nobody responded.

I tapped the ceiling above my head. "Whoever's up
there, come on down."

Shuffling sounds forged a path across the ceiling, made
the light in the center of the ceiling blip alarmingly, and
then culminated near the opening. When nothing popped
out, I poked the ceiling again. "Hello?"

Was that a sigh?

An oversized bare foot appeared in the opening,
followed by a hairy shin and then...

"Are those yoga pants?"

I was pretty sure I recognized those hairy legs, so when
the full Monty slid to the ground, I wasn't even surprised.

Not much anyway.

My ex stared at me with a grizzled and bruised face. His graying brown hair was tousled and customarily overlong. Spikes of hair stuck up on either side, as if he'd been grabbing it and pulling it away from his head. His usually pleasant features had a grayish cast that had my gaze skimming quickly to his shoulder. The telltale blood dotted the thin fabric of a light brown wife-beater tee-shirt. "What are you wearing?" I asked as I reached carefully to pull the fabric from the wound on his shoulder. Sure enough, King Henri's Tic-Tac-Toe logo stained his skin with blood.

Tom sighed. "I was naked when they grabbed me. When we got here they shoved me in a room and told me to get dressed in something. The pickins' were slim."

"They?" I asked, already knowing the answer.

He winced. "You wouldn't believe me if I told you."

Since my ex didn't know anything about my new job and life, I could see why he'd think that. "I'll believe more than you think. Spit it out, Tom."

He shook his head. The man was as stubborn as a tick on a hairless cat.

I sighed. Glancing at Elvo, I said, "Hey campfire breath, give the man a show."

Elvo's tail wagged with excitement. He lumbered to his big paws and shook himself, sending tufts of black fur flying around the room. I sucked in a tiny hairball before I saw it coming, and was coughing up my spleen when Tom made a sound of horror. I looked up to see the hound bristling with fire, from the tip of his flaming tail, to the top of his fiery nose. And Tom holding his fingers in the sign of a cross as if Elvo were a vampire.

Alrighty then.

"So, that's my partner, Elvo. He's a Hellhound. Well, mostly. I think there's some Pekinese in there or something."

Elvo chuffed out a laugh. Because Pekinese are smart.

"Seriously, Rae? This is your new job? Running around with dogs that set themselves on fire?"

I shrugged. "Technically, he sets other stuff on fire." I grinned at the big goof. "Isn't he cool?"

Elvo gave me soft eyes.

"What about me?" Justice asked, walking over to stand next to me. "Aren't you going to introduce me too?"

I eyed him up and down. "I'm glad to see you don't look ready to yark anymore."

He shrugged. "Give me a break, Traveler Kitt. It's not every day a man gets marked by a ghoul king."

I winced. "Yeah, about that..."

Justice stepped forward, offering Tom his hand. "My name's Justice. I'm Rae's partner."

Tom looked as if he was considering making the cross sign again. "What kind of partner?"

After a beat, Justice dropped his hand. "I'm her guide."

Tom snickered nastily. "I'll just bet you are. What kind of guidance do you think old Kitten here needs? I've already given her twenty years of that kind of guidance, if you know..."

I held up a hand. "Stop talking right now."

Tom opened his mouth again.

"Do not."

He closed it, worked his lips around for a bit and then opened them again.

I pulled out my knife. "Nope!"

When he finally seemed to get that I wasn't interested in his misogynistic fantasies, he shrugged and clamped his lips closed. I turned to speak to Justice. "You have no idea how you guys got here?"

"No. I have a vague memory of the ground falling out

from under me and then a cavern of some kind. Then some-body cut me and I woke up here."

When I glanced at Molly, she nodded. "That's pretty much what I remember too."

"You don't remember how you two got to this apartment?"

They both shook their heads.

"I have a theory for why we're *here*, though," Molly said. When we looked at her, she added, "I think Henri wanted you to find us after we were turned. He wanted us to turn you."

"The ultimate betrayal," Justice said, nodding. "From what I've heard about Henri, that sounds like him."

If that were true, it would explain why Tom was there too. I shook my head, disgusted. "How did I get so lucky?"

Molly shrugged. "Maybe he holds a grudge because you keep escaping his minions. Or maybe he likes you."

I snorted. "What about Juggler?"

"I haven't seen him for a while," Justice said, frowning. "Do you think the ghouls got him too?"

"It seems likely."

I thought about that, trying to pull all the pieces into a coherent shape. My gaze fell on Elvo. "What's with the Hell-hound? He's been leading us on all kinds of fruitless adventures."

Justice and Elvo shared a look. I'd seen them do that kind of thing before, but I wasn't sure what type of commu-nicating they engaged in. Finally, Justice shrugged. "He's been looking for us too. It's possible he didn't know any more than you did."

I frowned, not satisfied with that answer. "He couldn't scent you?"

"Our scents have changed from the marks," Tom said,

surprising me. When we all looked at him, he blinked. "I heard some of the less ghouly guys talking about it. They said Henri's been moving people around, sending them on weird missions, blowing stuff up. It's kind of a game for him. He apparently likes to create chaos."

"Well, he's certainly good at it," I mumbled.

"Have you learned anything useful about the ghouls?"

"Only that they're turning live bodies now," Justice answered.

I blinked, staring at him as my mind tried to catch up. He was right. I hadn't made the connection. "This mark is turning you?"

"I think it might be," Justice told me, his eyes filled with sorrow. "I think the king came to this dimension so he could turn non-magical humans and end up with minions who look and sound normal."

I thought about the potential for disaster that would cause. "Not good."

"No," he agreed.

I glanced over at Molly and found her sitting on the edge of the bed staring at her hands as if she'd never seen them before. Tears burned my eyes. I was going to lose my best friend. And Justice. Tom belched softly. And yes, even him. What would my daughter do without her father?

No. I couldn't let this happen. My daughter was *not* going to live in a world where monsters ruled. Not if I could help it. I jerked my gaze to Justice's sapphire eyes and fought the urge to scream and cry.

"What?" he asked softly. Justice lifted a warm, lightly calloused thumb to my jawline and branded the shape of my jaw with his heated touch. I closed my eyes and let myself lean closer, knowing my chance to make something special with him was quite possibly gone.

Gone before I'd even let myself really consider it.

Gone before I could reach out and test the possibilities.

Just...gone.

He shifted slightly and warmth bathed my entire front. I kept my eyes closed because I was afraid if I opened them, the moment would be gone. Or I'd see the monster in his eyes.

No! My eyes snapped open and I stepped away from him. I needed distance or I'd never be able to think. "What can we do to stop this?"

"Stop the change?"

"Yes. Fix you guys and all the other humans he's turned. And send Henri back where he belongs."

Justice's focus seemed to slip for a beat, his handsome face going soft, his gaze blank. A swirl of something foreign and ugly slipped through his eyes in the midst of that blankness and I had to tighten my hands into fists to keep from slapping at that unwelcome taint. But then he blinked and said, "The Travel Bureau."

That made me frown. It seemed such a random thing for him to say. "What about it?"

"Fair has..." He frowned, another vacant expression stealing his personality away.

"Fair has what?" I urged, my gaze avoiding his for fear of what I'd see. He stood there for a long moment, stiff and immobile. But then he seemed to shake himself. He reached for me, grabbing my arms in a too-tight grip. I fought the urge to complain and pull away.

"Look into my eyes, Rae," he said, and I almost laughed. "Are you trying to hypnotize and compel me like a vampire?"

He dipped his head and held my gaze as his grip tightened more. I winced. That was gonna leave a bruise. "Just keep your eyes on mine. Let me hold onto the humanity for long enough to tell you..."

I nodded, doing as he asked. "I'm right here, partner. Just hold on." Tears burned my eyes but I blinked them away. "Talk to me."

"Fair has a spray that might kill the ghoulish taint. It's very effective. But you need to use it before the victim is too far gone."

My pulse sped, suddenly terrified I'd already be too late. "How long is too long?"

The sapphire gaze softened slightly and I grabbed his arms, giving him a little shake. "Stay with me, Justice. What's my timetable?"

Awareness bleeding back into his eyes, Justice shook his head. "Hours. Maybe a couple of days. I don't know. But it's the only chance we've got."

"What happens to the victim if it's been too long?"

His gaze slid away, but I placed my hands on his face and pulled his attention back to me. "What happens?"

"They die."

Tears burned in my eyes.

"You'll need a lot of the stuff," Justice said. "Henri's made a lot of baby ghouls since he arrived."

I nodded. "Who will keep you safe while I'm gone?"

"We'll be fine."

He said it dismissively, but I'd seen him ambling along that ledge, and I didn't believe him. "No. You guys will hurt yourselves if I don't keep an eye on you."

Frustration flitted through him, making his sexy mouth tighten. "Rae, you need to get going. Let us take care of ourselves."

I shook my head.

"Woof!"

Justice and I glanced down at the big black Hellhound mutt draped over our shoes. "What?" I barked out. "We're kind of busy here."

Elvo's big body wriggled happily, his tail smacking my ankle. "Woof!"

Then I realized what he was trying to tell me. Elvo could stay with them. He could protect Justice and Mols until I came back with the spray. I nodded. "Okay, smoke breath. But if you let them hurt themselves you'll be dealing with me."

His happy tail still whipping, Elvo let his tongue loll out of the side of his face, making him look truly goofy. But fire rolled through the brown gaze.

Message received. I could almost hear him growl the words. *Bring it cupcake.*

"Elvo will stay..." My words trailed off as I looked into Justice's blank stare and pain pinched my chest. It was even worse when I looked at Molly, who sat with her mouth gaping, staring at nothing.

Unfortunately, Tom still looked lucid. He'd draped himself over the room's only bed and was waggling his brows at me. "What do ya say, Kitten? One for the road?"

The air vibrated on a growl.

Elvo raised canine brows at me.

I shook my head. "I'm going to see Fair, I told the dog. Hopefully, I'll be back in an hour or so. You hold down the fort here, k?"

Elvo gave my knee a lick in response.

"Ugh!" I rubbed the damp denim with a grimace.

Elvo jumped up and trotted over to Tom, who'd gone blank with his brows still in the upright and lecherous position. "Woof?"

I briefly considered his obvious question. It was a tough

one. Finally, I sighed. "I guess protect him too. But Molly and Justice are your key targets."

The big dog jumped onto the bed and draped himself over Tom, looking pleased with himself. I opened my mouth to object, knowing Tom was going to have puppies when he woke up again and realized a giant dog was pinning him to the bed. Then I smiled.

Karma's a wild woman with revenge in her heart. And she just became my best friend.

I thought about Aere and tried to form a bounce before remembering the stadium was warded against traveling. Panic dug clawed fingers into my chest before I realized I had another way out of that cursed place.

"Thank you crazy housewife," I said as I took off running.

16

LIKE A BAD PORN STAR

I approached the equipment shed in the back corner of the property at a run, my head on a swivel for more of Henri's surprises. As I ran, I scanned the fencing near the corner, looking for the opening the housewife turned baby ghoul had described. Since daylight had given way to night a few minutes previous, seeing anything in the shadowed length of chain link was a challenge.

A low growl behind me was my first and only warning that I was no longer alone.

I whipped around and spotted the low forms of two ghouls shambling in my direction, their eyes like small, hot coals in the growing darkness.

My blade was in one hand, my gun in the other as I stepped forward to meet them. Sitting back and waiting for trouble just wasn't my style. Besides, I had things to do.

I was running full out by the time I fired my gun. I'd aimed for the ghoul's ear and missed, the bullet slamming into the thing's skull three inches above its ear. I did a mental shrug. It hadn't been a bad shot in the darkness and on the move.

The impact slammed the nasty creature around and it staggered sideways several steps. Meanwhile, the second ghoul was coming at me with claws slashing and teeth snapping.

I shot it in the groin and slashed at it as I hit the ground and rolled away, coming up stretched on my belly with the gun in two hands.

The harsh bark of gunfire bit the night. The monster jerked backward with each concussion, finally spinning around and slamming face-first into the grass. It hadn't even tried to catch itself.

A good sign.

But I wasn't going to be fooled into thinking the monster was dead-dead. Ghouls, I was learning, were the monster dimension's cockroaches. Hard to kill and always scurrying around in the shadows.

Ghoul number two was lumbering my way, moaning like a bad porn star. I jumped to my feet and holstered my gun. If I wanted to finish this before dawn lit the sky I'd have to get up close and personal. I grimaced at the thought. With a sigh, I ran right at it, blade high and out to the side of my body. I slammed into the ghoul and braced my left arm beneath its nasty clacking jaws to keep it from biting me as I attempted to slice the vein by its gristly ear. But the monster had no intention of letting me dispatch it. Its head swung from side to side, trying to dislodge my arm while slashing at my exposed back. I'd known that was going to be a problem, but I only had two arms and I'd planned to move fast. Wriggling away from its slicing claws as best I could, I made three sloppy cuts near the ear, unable to find the right spot and get the depth I needed for the wound.

Agony sliced down my back as the ghoul's claws found me. I screamed, the sound ending in a growl of pure irritation. I lifted the blade and slashed it down, finally severing the ear. As the ghoul roared in pain, I slammed my blade to the hilt in the thick vein and jumped off as it began to bleed.

The ghoul reached for me as I climbed to my feet. I kicked it hard in the jaw and danced away from its attack.

Turning around, I started hobbling toward the fence. Heavy footfalls pounded into the grass behind me. I growled, but didn't even have time to swear before the first ghoul slammed into me. I landed in the grass with the thing riding my back.

It was a really bad spot to be. The monster was small and wizened, looking like old boot leather that had been left too long in the sun. There couldn't be a cup full of liquid left inside its spidery body. But it felt like it weighed a thousand pounds. I knew that was probably because I was tired and hadn't had anything to eat or drink for over a day. But, sweet cherubs on a crescent moon, I just needed one thing to go my way.

Just one.

I snapped an elbow into the snarling baseball-headed thing on my back, knocking it away for the space of a single heartbeat.

A full moon peeked out from behind the line of mature trees bordering the field. The silver light painted the grass and illuminated a dark slash in the fencing I could see from my lower-profile position.

Silver lining.

If only I could get rid of the giant cockroach on my back.

Snapping teeth found my shoulder and crunched down hard. I screamed as agony twisted through me. Moonlight slipped behind a cloud as I struggled to dislodge my unwelcome rider. It slipped back in time to glint off something in the grass.

In shear desperation, I reached toward whatever it was, hoping I could use it as a weapon. My hand folded over a firm, warm length of metal. My eyes went wide.

My right arm had grown numb beneath the ghoul's determined gnashing but I could use my left in a pinch. I'd practiced shooting with both hands when I was a cop.

With a snap of my wrist, I opened the fan-like blade. Digging my toes into the grass, I shoved as hard as I could, in the hopes of dislodging the leathery cockroach. I did manage to unbalance him and was able to roll away, but he reached for me before I could get clear, snagging my ankle in his nasty claws.

Fresh pain seared along my leg but I didn't have the breath to scream. Instead, I swung Justice's magic blade and sliced off the ghoul's hand. It snatched the torn limb back with a rusty scream and I rolled to my feet. Another clawed hand found my ankle. I sliced that hand off too.

The thing was thrashing wildly at my feet as I bent over it and rested the blade against its gristly, wrinkled throat. "Home run," I said as I sliced with every bit of strength I had left, severing its nasty head from its neck. "Game over."

Panting and in pain, I stepped away, eying the dark slash in the fence as I stumbled forward. The fence seemed a mile away as I stumbled toward it, my gaze on a swivel looking for more ghouls. When I finally arrived at the breach, I wasted no time ducking through. Hurrying along the fence line with Justice's blade clutched in one hand and my gun in the other, I kept my head low and tried to keep my steps light and quick.

Given how I felt, that was no easy task.

At least I had a pretty good idea who'd been tied up in the equipment shed. Justice's knife being there couldn't have been a coincidence.

I stopped near the street, just inside the tree line, and eyed the few humans moving near the front gate. They looked normal. Acted like normal humans. But I was no longer sure who was ghoul and who wasn't. As nasty as the glow-eyed nightmarish version of the ghouls were, at least I knew what I was working with, and where they were vulnerable.

The happy housewife had caught me off guard. And I'd seen with my own eyes how unpredictable marked humans could be.

I shuddered at the memory of Justice walking along that narrow ledge. And the fear in Molly's eyes. And Tom... I shook my head. Even as a potential ghoul that man was just annoying and pathetic.

The soft crack of a stick breaking under a shoe had me ducking into the trees, my hand tightening around the blade. My heart pounded hard against my ribs and I suddenly felt a little dizzy, my poor body starved of resources for too long. I'd been running on pure adrenaline.

I took long, slow breaths and released them just as slowly, trying for calm.

The man emerging from the trees was big and burly. His face was round, his cheeks and chin lost within a fall of dark, frizzy hair. The beard reached to his chest and was unruly, tangled with sticks. But it was the dark smears around his mouth and on his hands that had me wanting to run screaming into the night.

Blood.

"Hey!" a deep voice called out.

I jerked in surprise, afraid the cop who was hurrying down the street in my direction had somehow spotted me. But his gaze was on the burly guy. And when the ghoul stepped out of the shadows into the illumination of the street lights, the cop lifted his gun.

My mind played a video of what was about to happen. The cop would demand that the ghoul stop. He might even fire his gun when the burly guy ignored his command. But the bullets wouldn't matter. He didn't know the creature's vulnerable areas. By the time he started shooting, it would be too late.

Unfortunately, it all happened just as I predicted, playing out over the next thirty seconds. Fast. Too fast. So fast that, by the time I ran in the cop's direction, he'd already been taken to the ground by the baby ghoul.

I had just a heartbeat to look into the cop's young, terrified face with a look of regret, before I sliced Justice's blade across the ghoul's throat.

The cop stared at the head as it arced away into the night, hitting the road with a meaty splat. And then he turned his horror-filled gaze to me.

I knew he was going to start screaming. I had two seconds to get to him. To stop him. But I couldn't. I needed to get to Fair. I started backing away. "These are ghouls. You have to cut off their heads." I didn't have time to get into the other ways to kill them. There wasn't time. And he wouldn't believe me anyway.

His lips moved a few times and then opened wide, as he dug for his gun and began to scream for me to stop.

But I'd already pulled my bounce around me, and was stepping out into a dry, bruising wind, in the Aero dimension.

17

LIKE A CATEGORY FIVE HURRICANE

I'd expected to land in my usual spot, in the middle of a large flat swath of crisp, brown grass. I'd expected to find myself alone in that brown vastness, looking out on a long, low-slung structure that was half buried in the earth to protect it from the endless winds—the scouring, brutal bite of air that was a constant challenge in the Aere dimension.

I'd expected to have a second to gather myself...to prepare for what I needed to do.

But what I got instead was a small, squarish woman with wild orange hair, pale skin, and a determined look on her round windburned face.

Fair.

I jumped, made a small noise that wasn't very manly, and said, "Oh!"

"I know why you're here, and I'm coming back with you." The med tech's dark orange eyebrows stretched into determined slashes on her face, telling me she wasn't going to be easily talked out of what she intended. Her ruddy cheeks deepened in color under my regard, and I noted the way she twined her work-worn hands in front of her.

"What's wrong?" I asked, taking a step toward the other woman. "You look terrified."

Fair shook her head and spun on a sensible brown shoe. "Come with me. We don't have much time."

I opened my mouth to argue, but Fair was quickly putting distance between us. She moved like a stalking big cat, sturdy legs stretching to eat up the ground. I had no choice but to follow. Breaking into jog, I reached her just before she opened the door, grabbing her arm. "Fair, whatever you want help with, I need to take care of something else first. It's a matter of life or death."

Fair jerked her arm away from me and said, "Not here. Let's go to my office."

Her quick, determined strides didn't ease as we entered the strange building that was the Travel Bureau, a paranormal governing body of sorts, which had its metaphorical finger on the pulse of everything happening in all the dimensions. I hadn't asked a lot of questions when Justice had brought me there before...I'd been too wrapped up in my own situation to give it much thought. I realized that had been a mistake. There were likely resources at the Bureau that would make my life as a Traveler easier.

But, judging by Fair's tight expression, and her headlong rush to her office, I figured it wasn't the right time to ask for a tour and an overview of the Bureau's offerings.

"Bright morning to you Fair."

Fair mumbled something and swept past the woman in the hallway, whose questioning blue-green gaze slid to me at her workmate's unusual brusqueness. I smiled and gave her a little wave, hurrying after Fair.

I'd barely stepped through the door into a small, white

room before the door slammed shut behind me. I swung around in surprise and saw Fair with her hand still on the lock she'd just turned.

"Fair, talk to me. What's going on?"

Like ice cream in the summer, she seemed to melt before my eyes. Her determined expression ran down her face and puddled around her chin. A shininess I'd never witnessed before in her eyes gave me a jolt. Were those tears?

"Anil's been taken."

Anil was the guy who ran the Bureau. He'd been helpful to me in the past and seemed like a good guy. But the obvious depths of Fair's distress said there was more to her mood... I gasped in realization. "You and Anil?"

Some of the determined belligerence returned to her expression and she squared her shoulders. "And why not? Do you think I'm unlovable?"

My lips flapped for a bit under the whiplash bite of her changing emotions. She'd taken my question to a dark place really fast. "Um. No. Of course not." I bit my tongue against the need to tell her I was questioning whether her *boyfriend* was loveable. Somehow I couldn't picture Anil twisting the sheets in a fit of passion.

Blech. I shook my head, trying to shake off the visions dancing in my head like sugar plums. "Okay, tell me what happened."

"He went to the Terro...Earth...dimension and the ghoul king got him."

I blinked in surprise. "Why would Anil go there? Especially now?"

She shrugged. "He visits all the dimensions regularly. It's part of his job. He usually just does a quick check-in with his contacts and then comes home. But this time..." She sniffed loudly, scraping a pale hand over the tears wetting her face.

My first thought was...why Anil? With my second thought nipping at the first one's heels. It was kind of handy that Fair's problem intersected with mine. Then I thought about what a jerk I was for even thinking of that when Fair and apparently her boyfriend Anil...blech...were in distress.

"Okay. Long story short," I told her, "I'm in the same situation. That's why I've come. Justice, Juggler, and Molly were taken too. I've come to see if you have anything to unghoul somebody?"

Fair's face twisted in thought. "Unghoul?"

I flapped my hands in frustration. "The king is creating ghouls that look just like people. They haven't even died. He's putting this..." I tapped my fingertips against my shoulder... "magical mark on them and they become ghouls."

Fair walked over to the narrow bed against the back wall and dropped heavily onto it, her knees seeming to turn soft beneath her. "That's why he was taken," she mumbled. "With Anil under his control, Henri could gain command of the Travel Bureau and, through its connections, all the dimensions."

I looked around the room and located a white leather chair in front of a white desk and shook my head. "Really..." I said, grimacing. "I realize it's not a good time to ask but..." I swept my arm around the space. "What's with all the white? It's a bit overwhelming."

Fair didn't seem to hear me. She was deep inside her own head.

Rolling the chair over to the bed, I sat down right in front of her, our knees almost touching. My faded jeans and charcoal gray t-shirt seemed almost garish in the monochromatic room, making me feel like some kind of invader.

Reaching out, I clasped her hand, finding it cold, the fingers lightly calloused. "Fair. I really need your help. Do you think you can pull it together and develop something to stop Henri and save our friends?"

Fair didn't respond. I gave her hand a slight tug. "Fair? Don't leave me alone here. If I go into your lab and start mixing stuff up by myself, your lab's going to look like a category five hurricane came through it within minutes. I wouldn't do it intentionally. I'm just a messy cook. Lissy laughs at me all the time about it. She thinks I do it to get out of cooking. She's partly right, but, well, cooking's not my best thing..." I trailed off, realizing I was blathering.

Fair blinked and jerked her gaze to mine. "I think I might have something that will work." She jumped off the bed and was out the door before I could open my mouth to ask what she had.

"I thought I'd lost you there for a minute," I said, laughing as we basically ran down the pristine corridors. "Your expression was like a blinking cursor on a computer screen. Blink, blink, blink. Then you just snapped out of it with a solution. I guess brains work differently here in Aere, huh? Maybe from all that wind abrasion you must suffer as kids."

"You're babbling again," Fair said, shoving open a white door that looked like a dozen others in the hallway and storming inside. "I thought it was okay when your nonsensical blathering was helping me think, but now it's just annoying."

Alrighty then.

"Out!" she yelled at two scientists who were dressed in the customary white coats with an array of test tubes filling carriers in front of them.

"Out. Shoo. Go!" Fair ushered the two scientists out

when they hesitated, trying to collect their vials before they left. "Leave them!"

The two scurried out, sending surprised glances back toward Fair and me. Clearly they'd never been yelled at like that before. They should hang around in my neighborhood for a while. Mr. Nodges next door was like the neighborhood trash can Nazi. He threatened once to paint a rectangle on the drive where I should put my trash can on pickup days. Apparently, my can touched his once and he nearly blew his knickers over it.

He never painted that rectangle. It's possible I showed him my gun in its holster. I didn't draw it. Just indulged in a little show and quell.

Oops, I was still blabbering.

I shook myself out of my memories and looked up to find Fair flinging things around the lab. At first I thought she was in destructive mode, but then I realized she was looking for something. "Can I help?"

"No. I... Aha!" She came up hard and fast, banging her head on the cabinet door frame. "Ouch!"

I winced. That had sounded like it hurt.

Rubbing the back of her head, Fair held a large glass object connected to a rubber tube with a ball on the end. It looked like a giant perfume bottle. An ugly one. "What's that?"

She caressed the object, looking a little less afraid. "This is what's going to save our friends." Her voice broke and tears slipped down her ruddy cheeks again, dripping onto the floor.

I felt the urge to say something, though I knew that whatever I said would sound empty or dishonest. Her priorities and mine didn't exactly mesh. Though they were close.

"What can I do to help?" I gently urged. "I don't think we have a lot of time."

She blinked rapidly, nodding. "Sorry. I can't seem to stop crying since..." She sniffed hard and put her hands on the giant atomizer. "Years ago, there was a magically-induced plague breakout on Igne dimension. I was tasked with creating an antidote for the disease. But we had a problem because, as you know, most of the residents on that plane are monsters, or monster adjacent. We needed a way to medicate without touch or even getting too close to the victims. It was a seemingly impossible task until I created this baby."

I lifted my brows at the thing. It looked as if it was the result of a second-grade science fair project.

"Don't underestimate the tool, Traveler Kitt," Fair said. "I saved an entire dimensional population with it."

Biting back a frustrated retort, I said, "Okay, so we have the delivery system. But what about the most important part?"

She looked at me as if I'd failed kindergarten on a scholarship. "Haven't you been listening? I developed an anti-magic serum already. We learned our lessons on Igne and are better prepared. I have enough in stock to save another dimension."

Hope soared on pretty pink wings. "It will nullify the king's mark?"

"It's the same concept, right? A magically induced taint. A spray that kills magically-induced taints." She shrugged, palms up as if asking how I could be so stupid.

That was easy. I'd had a lifetime of practice.

"Okay then. Perfect. Where's the stuff? I'll grab it and we can go."

Of course it wasn't quite that easy. As Fair worked, three

more scientists crept into the room. One of them, a tall, dark-haired man with a perfect jawline and a probing yellow gaze skimmed a dismissive look over me before settling his gaze on Fair. "What do you, Citizen Fair?"

Fair was back to rifling through the cabinets, her wild, orange hair bobbing around just above the counter. "Nothing do I," she told him. My internal grammar checker exploded in my head, trying to make sense. Were they speaking an alien form of pig Latin?

"With us come. Things many we talk must."

"Nope." Fair popped up with a large rubber container, which looked like a Tupperware container for cake and had a white lid. "Involve not yourself. Away yourself take."

A small woman with stick-straight dark hair that fell in vertical lines to her chin, said something in another language. Fair responded, a bite in her voice.

I didn't a word understand.

Fair shoved the ugly perfume bottle at me and pushed me toward the door. "I will deal with this," she told her peers. "Please go back to work."

The dark-haired man shook his head. "Know must Anil."

Fair kept walking, her jaw tight as she shoved me through the door. "Anil knows. I'm doing this project for him. Super-secret. Need to know and all that." Fair closed the door behind us with more force than I'd ever seen from her. She'd always been calm and gentle around me.

Clearly, she was stressed.

"What was that about?" I asked, reaching for my blade as Fair took off running toward the door at the end of the hall.

"Just run," she said.

Behind us, the door to the lab swung open. "Halt!"

Fair picked up the pace, her thick legs pumping like pistons. "Hurry, Traveler!"

She hit the back door as something gelatinous splatted the metal just above her head. "Ah!"

She wore a look of such terror, it rubbed off on me. I yanked my gun from its holster and swung around just as another purple gelatinous thing slammed into my chest. It hit with the force of a bullet and I stumbled backward, falling through the door Fair was holding open.

She slammed it closed as soon as I cleared, then rushed over when I hit the ground. "Come on, Traveler. We need to bounce."

My chest was on fire. My legs felt as if they had knives in them. And the world was blurry, as if I were looking through glasses with petroleum jelly on the lenses. My head felt as if it had exploded when I tried to sit up. "Ah," I moaned, falling back to the ground.

Behind the door we'd just exited through, footsteps pounded. Around us, wind whipped and tore at everything in its path. The only thing that saved us was the fact that we were on the ground and therefore presented a low profile. But even so, a trio of dirt devils scoured toward us, flinging choking dust into the air as they spun.

Fair grabbed at me, her expression frantic. "Come on!" She yanked hard enough to pry my upper body off the ground, but she couldn't hold me. I was a hundred and thirty-mmpff pounds of Rae-shaped jelly. "I...ca..."

Each word took seconds to emerge from my mouth. It was frustrating.

Pounding started nearby. I rolled my well-oiled gaze to the door and saw some kind of blurry stick jammed under the knob. "Go, Fff...Ffff..." I tried to give Fair a thumb's up and poked myself in the nostril. "Ow. That hur...hur..."

"Seven suns in Septum's sky," Fair exclaimed. "We'll have to get creative."

"Septum? I once ha..ha...d a deviated septum and it was bbbaaaa..." I frowned, losing the last word entirely. I clasped the edge of my nostril and moved it back and forth. "I think it's o...o..." I frowned again.

"Get ready to bounce," Fair told me. "Sorry about this." Without warning she threw herself on top of me, wrapping her pale, lightly freckled arms around my waist and squeezing hard. "Go!" she yelled into my ear.

"Ah!" I objected, my hands flapping around my head. "What are you do...do...? *Sweet Cherubs on a blood red moon.* "I'm not that kind of g...g..."

"Bounce, girl!" Fair screamed into my face.

In my wounded delirium, I wondered if she was thinking about biting me.

The door slammed open. Mr. Perfect Jaw with the backward speech stepped out into the biting wind, a purple plastic gun pointed right at me.

More crazy jelly! "Not do you that!" I tried to yell. The words got caught in the wind and were yanked away.

"Bounce!" Fair yelled again.

I attempted to grab a thought. Someplace familiar that was away from...

Splat!

The poisonous little jiggly dart hit the dirt an inch from my ear. I closed my eyes and formed a picture in my mind. And the world shifted around me.

18

THIS ISN'T WHAT IT LOOKS LIKE

I landed hard, my back slamming painfully onto a concrete sidewalk and my head smacking against grass. I groaned loudly, feeling as if a boulder sat on my chest.

Then the boulder moved and my eyes popped open, seeing a familiar round face mere inches from mine. "Fair? What are you doing?" I grunted as I tried to shift out from under her. "I can't breathe."

Someone gasped and we jerked our gazes toward the woman standing a few feet away, an enormous yellow and white tabby cat hanging limply from her slender arms.

"Um," my next-door neighbor said, skimming an embarrassed look over Fair before looking away. "Sorry to interrupt..." She shifted the cat into a slightly better hold. "Manus got out again. I swear every time he does he gains five pounds."

"It's the pizza place down the street," I said.

My neighbor, whose name I could never remember said, "Huh?"

"They feed him leftovers. He loves pepperoni pizza." My

voice was coming out breathy from having my lungs compressed.

"Ah. Okay. Well..." She started to turn toward the door of her apartment and seemed to decide against it. "Look, Rae. I'm as non-judgmental as the next girl. I don't care who you want to date." She slid another look over Fair and almost grimaced, but she stopped the expression before it fully formed. "But maybe you could keep your...assignations private? That's why the good Lord made apartments. AmIright?" Her laugh was small and tight and heat flushed my cheeks. "This isn't..." I realized before I said the words what they would sound like to my neighbor. *This isn't what it looks like,* said every cheating man or woman ever.

The neighbor's name was Sissy, I thought. Or maybe Marissa. What did it matter? I knew Manus. He and I had shared pizza many times. He was more interesting than his owner. He liked to see the world...mix it up with strangers and friends alike. He was a cool cat.

I grinned at that thought.

"Have a nice night," I finally said, shoving my way clear of Fair's seemingly frozen form. "'Night, Manus."

"Meow!" The big cat gave me pleading eyes over his owner's shoulder and I made the "call me" sign with my fingers, mouthing *Call me.*

Yeah, it was possible I was still suffering the aftereffects of the jelly bullets.

"What did she mean about assignations?" Fair asked. She was checking out the atomizer, probably to make sure it hadn't broken in the bounce. I knew the cake container had made it. I could feel the shape of it bruised into my ribs.

I sighed. "Nothing."

Fair looked around. "Where are we? Is Anil here?"

I certainly hoped not.

"No, we're at my apartment. I need to get a few things before we head to the stadium. It will only take a minute."

Five minutes later, we were trudging down the street after I realized my car wasn't there. Again. I couldn't call Molly for a ride, for obvious reasons. The only other option was...

I shook my head. The idea was unthinkable.

I. Just. Couldn't.

Calling for a drive share would also be ill conceived because I didn't want to draw any other human types into Henri's ever-widening net.

Three blocks later, Fair swiped a sleeve over her cheeks with a groan. "Why is it so hot on Terro. You need wind."

"Not like you live with, thank you very much."

"How much further is it?"

"Only a mile," I said under my breath. The stadium actually wasn't that far from my apartment. Especially when I had four tires and an engine under me.

"A mile!" she shrieked. "I can't. I'll expire."

I glanced over at her for the first time and alarm slammed into me. The med tech looked terrible. Her skin was all pasty, even her ruddy cheeks were more pink than red. The wild tangle of orange hair hung in wet strings around her face and neck. Her lips were pinched tightly together. I clasped her arms. "What's wrong, Fair? Are you sick?" I glanced in horror at the ugly perfume jar. "Is there something poisonous in that thing?"

She took a deep breath and scrubbed her wet face and neck with the wide sleeves of her lab coat. "I'm not sick. It's just that the air is so still here on Terro. And..." her gaze skipped away from me with embarrassment. "I don't usually walk very much."

I thought about that statement and her job at the Travel

Bureau. About the bed I'd seen in her office. Then I realized. "You *live* at the Bureau."

She chewed her bottom lip. "Yeah. Anil does too. And a couple of others."

"Like Dr. Jelly Darts?"

She curled her lip. "Unfortunately."

Suddenly, it all made sense to me. Fair likely never left the Bureau building. The only exercise she probably ever got was walking from the lab to the dining room. If there was a dining room. "Okay, well. If we walked slower, would that help?"

My phone rang before she could respond. I groaned aloud when I saw who it was. I stabbed the phone to answer. "You," I growled out.

"Where is she, Kitt? What have you gotten her into now?"

I might have snarled a little. "First of all, I didn't get her into anything. Her stupid boyfriend did. All I've been doing is trying to keep her out of it."

"Tell me where she is. I'm coming for her."

I barely kept from laughing. Rog was hardly an action hero. He considered himself under attack if a butterfly fluttered too close to his lunch at the park.

"Yeah? I'm so relieved. You can beat back the bugs while I'm fighting ghouls. That way, you know, I won't get distracted or accidently suck a fly up my nose."

Fair frowned.

"Why I oughta..." Rog responded.

"You oughta stay out of this and let me save Molly. I'm working on it right now."

There was a short silence, during which I considered hanging up. But then Rog sighed. His combative tone disappeared. "Let me help, Rae. Please. Molly's my best friend. I don't know what I'd do if something happened to her."

I don't know if his plea got to me because I felt the same way, or because we needed a ride to the stadium. Since I didn't want to believe I was that shallow, I went with option number one. "Okay. You can help. I need a ride."

"Where are you?"

I gave Rog our location and hung up. Pointing Fair to a redwood and iron bench under a tree, I was alarmed to see her all but collapse onto it. Seeing her mop at her sweat with wet sleeves, I was grateful the sun was down. The woman looked as if she might expire any second.

To distract her from dying, I asked, "So what's the deal with Dr. Jelly Gun?"

Fair blew a raspberry, which was apparently the multi-dimensional sign for disgust. "He's been gunning for Anil's job for decades."

"Pun intended?" I asked, slightly alarmed. Hopefully it wasn't always like the Okay Jelly Corral at the Bureau.

Fair shrugged. "He spies on everything Anil does and always tries to get him in trouble with the dimensional leaders."

"Is it working?"

She chewed her bottom lip. "Mostly no. But the Igne Chancellor doesn't like Anil and he could stir the rest of them up if he decided to. That's why Anil came to Terro during this dangerous time. He's trying to enhance his profile."

I bit back a sarcastic response, knowing it wouldn't be well received. But my personal opinion was that Anil had been monumentally stupid to put everyone at risk by getting himself captured. "Why'd Dr. Jelly Gun attack us?"

"He knows about me and Anil. We've been very discreet,

but..." She shrugged. "He knows that pinning something on me will taint Anil too." Fair fell into a glum silence and I was left to my own musings.

I paced while waiting for Rog to arrive, ready to pop a gasket by the time his bright yellow electric car buzzed up to the curb like a giant bumblebee. I wrenched the door open. "What took you so long?"

He glared at me with bugged-out brown eyes. "You're welcome, *Kitt*." He always said my name as if it were a steaming pile of biological waste on his tongue.

"We're going to the stadium." I climbed inside and Rog hit the...what? Battery? Not the gas. It had to be...the pedal. I did a mental head shake to clear my mental meanderings before they made me crazy. We oozed away from the curb at a speed my great grandmother Nana could have beaten with her cane.

A heartbeat later, I yelled, "Stop!"

The giant bumblebee jolted to a stop. "What?" Rog exclaimed. "Oh my goddess, Rae. If I broke my brakes because you startled me, you're paying to replace them."

I rolled my eyes. "If the car can't take a hard stop now and then, what good is it?"

He stared belligerently at me. The car was new and he was very proud of it. Which was why I'd been teasing him about it for days.

I shook my head and climbed out of the car, looking back at Fair. She was still sitting on the bench. Her eyes wide and unblinking, pointed in my direction.

"Are you coming?"

Her hands twitched atop the giant atomizer. "Um. What is that?"

I followed her gaze toward the bumblebee. "Think of it as a ride-on toy for adults."

She gave a little head shake. "I can't go with you. I've never ridden inside such a contraption."

I was pretty sure there had been vehicles on Aere when I'd gone there before. But maybe not the same kind of vehicles. "This runs on electricity. It can barely make it to the end of the street without a charge. We might have to plug it into a light pole or something to make it to the stadium. Trust me, as slow as Rog drives this thing, you wouldn't even get a hangnail if we bumped into something. You'll be fine."

"Very funny, Kitt," Rog called out. "I'm about to leave your butt behind."

I grinned. I didn't really think electric cars sucked lemons. I just liked tugging on Rog's last nerve. It was kind of a hobby.

Fair chewed her bottom lip, frowning at the small car.

"It's this or walking," I reminded her.

That did it. She fairly shot to her feet and ambled in my direction, her wilted lab coat sagging around her legs as she walked. I noticed for the first time that she wore tall, white socks that disappeared above the hem of her dress, which—lock up all the kids—was cream-colored instead of white. I grinned at her as she approached, wanting so badly to tease her about the wild color addition. But she was already a mess and I figured she might take it wrong. I only mean-teased Rog. And only because he gave as good as he got.

When we were all settled, with me scrunched in the back of the little car and Fair pale and shuddering in the front, Rog once again oozed away from the curb. Fair's initial jolt of alarm was soon soothed into a coma-like state as we crawled past buildings and were outrun by squirrels along the route.

"Why the stadium?" Rog asked.

I told him where we'd found Molly and Justice.

"The closest gate is the front one."

I shook my head. "We can't use the front. There are fake humans everywhere out there. Just buzz slowly on by like everything's normal and we'll go in the way I came out."

Rog nodded and the car fell silent for a moment as he crept closer to the stadium. He looked over at his passenger a beat later. "Hi, Fair."

She twitched and turned her head very slowly, as if she were afraid the car might capsize if she moved too quickly. "Hello."

"Do you remember me?"

I rolled my eyes. "Of course she remembers you," I said. "Then again, you *were* shaped like a Macy's Thanksgiving Day parade balloon at the time."

Rog had had an unfortunate encounter with a sea monster and had come away feeling a little bloated. As in dead in the water for several days kind of bloated. He'd been nearly unrecognizable.

Fair had tended to him night and day until he'd pulled through. I knew that because I'd been sitting by his bed the entire time.

Fair, being nicer than I...imagine that...smiled at Rog. "I do remember. How are you doing? You're looking well."

Rog smiled back and I grudgingly admitted to myself that he wasn't a bad looking guy when he wasn't glowering. "I'm good." He laughed. "I really enjoyed being Zorro for a while after that healing. Any chance you can give me a magic booster?"

Rog had temporarily gained the ability to use a blade fairly effectively after his magical healing infusions. He was clearly hoping to regain that ability. Being a small guy at five six or so, and kind of skinny, he'd likely been a 90-pound weakling growing up. The constant butt of jokes.

That thought made me feel bad for teasing him.

"Sorry. No Zorro for you," Fair said, not a hint of humor in her voice.

Rog deflated.

A block later, we ducked through a loose barrier and drove past the Wasp Stadium's front gate. There were half a dozen inhuman, leathery ghouls with glowing red eyes shuffling around among a bunch of cops and people in suits and skirts who didn't seem to notice or mind.

Obviously, all of those people had been changed. My chest suddenly felt heavy and my breathing constricted. How far had Henri's diabolical plan progressed?

Fair's eyes were bulging.

Rog kept making choking noises as if he were trying to hack up a hairball. "Rae?"

"It's nothing," I lied. "We're good. Nobody even glanced at us when we drove by. This is going to be a piece of cake." I was such a lying liar who lies. Pointing to a broken street light a block ahead, I said, "Pull your car under that lamp and kill the engine. We'll get out there." I turned to Rog. "Drive straight home, lock all your doors, and don't let anybody in for any reason. Got it?"

Rog ignored me and opened the door, stepping out onto the curb.

I leaped out my side. "Roger!"

He shook his head. "I'm coming, Rae. I already told you that."

"No! It's dangerous. Did you see those things back there? They'll literally eat your face if they catch you. I'm not using that word hyperbolically. I mean *literally*."

"I'm coming," Rog insisted. "You can either stand out here arguing with me all night, or we can go save Molly."

Closing my eyes, I counted to ten, willing my temper to

soothe and my pulse to calm. Then I gave up. There was no reason at all to be calm. And every reason to ride the adrenaline wave that was currently swamping me. Opening my eyes again, I looked at Fair. "Do you have everything you need?"

She nodded, her eyes still uncomfortably wide.

"Okay. Let's go." I took off running toward the fence line, which was bordered by a mix of old-growth evergreens and deciduous trees. The narrow path beneath my feet was covered in early-falling leaves, as well as pine needles and the occasional pine cone that threatened to break my ankle. The needles sent the soothing scent of pine into the air, an incongruous thing in a dark night that was filled with monsters.

As I ran, I became slowly aware of a hoarse wheezing sound behind me and realized what it was. I jolted to a stop, Roger slamming painfully into me. "Ouch! Rog."

He stepped back, hands up. "Warn a guy before you stop. I was in the groove."

I was sure he was. Running was kind of Rog's thing. Especially *away* from messes at work. He could win marathons if somebody just put a mess to clean up at the starting line.

I would have said as much, but when I glanced at our companion I lost the ability to speak.

19

I CAN SMELL STALE BEER AND SWEAT

Fair was way behind us on the path. She was doubled over with her hands on her knees, sounding like she might throw up. She'd dropped her magical medicine and its ugly dispenser on the path in front of her and her chest heaved from over-exertion.

"Fair? I'm so sorry. I forgot you're not a runner."

As I reached her she toppled sideways and I barely caught her before she slammed into the tree with her head. "Whoa," I said, easing her to the ground. She lay on her back and spread her arms as if to give her lungs more room to fill.

Fair couldn't speak for a couple of minutes. When the heaving had abated, she looked up at me with tears in her eyes. "Maybe you should go on ahead without me."

I shook my head. "No. You want to see Anil again, right?" It was dirty pool and I knew it. But our best chance of saving everyone was with Fair. And she'd never forgive herself if her dropping out ended up cursing Anil to life, or death, as a monster. "Just take a few minutes. We'll walk the rest of the way."

Her grimace reminded me that she didn't like walking much better than she did running.

I tried not to pace or look impatient as Fair did what I suggested. She lay on the ground looking like a ruby-faced snow angel for several minutes, until she had the energy to push herself to a seated position. "Okay. Let's go."

The med tech was still redder in the face than was healthy, but I gave her points for wanting to keep going. I helped her stand and then handed the diffuser to Rog. I took the tray of magical meds, relieving Fair of carrying anything but herself.

Rog fell back to her side and started talking to her in low tones. He soon had her laughing with his stories of his and my battles at The Muddle and I smiled. Not only in remembering those battles, but because the stories seemed to keep Fair from remembering that she was out of her depth.

I made a mental note to take the annoying assistant out to lunch after we'd quelled the ghoul rebellion. To thank him for being a decent human being.

"Here's the breach," I whispered back to them.

The smile on Fair's face fell away and she frowned, looking suddenly very serious. "We need to find a high spot where we can disperse the antidote," she told me.

Holding the cut in the fencing wide for her and Rog to sneak through, I said, "I have just the spot." When we were all inside the fence, I signaled them to hang back and did a quick recon of the area. The shed was still empty and there were no ghouls in the vicinity. Rog poked his head inside the shed as I was finishing up. "Ah, this stuff brings back memories."

My brows arced into my hairline. "You used to be a farmer?"

He shook his head. "I was in charge of managing the fields in a ball park before I came to work for Molly."

I nudged him out the door in front of me. "I did not know that. Why'd you quit?"

He shrugged. "It was hard work and I had other interests."

"Fashion?"

He whipped a look my way, looking for sarcasm. There wasn't any mockery in my expression or my tone, so he shrugged. "I know it's weird, but I've always been interested in clothes. My mama used to dress me up when I was a kid and I enjoyed how happy it made everybody to see me in my little suits and caps." He laughed. "I guess I equated fashion with happiness."

"Makes sense." I turned as Fair joined us, pointing toward the tower in the distance. "That's our destination." Sharpening my gaze on her, I said, "You'll have to climb some steps."

She deflated again, then nodded. "I can do it."

I wrapped an arm around her and squeezed. "Let's go. I'd like to get out of the open as fast as possible."

Limited by Fair's slow, stumbling jog, my hope of getting out of the open quickly died. Rog and I had slowed to a walk and still found ourselves stopping several times and waiting for the med tech to catch up. Fair's round face was red enough from her efforts that I could see the color even through the night. Her forehead glistened with sweat and her breathing was labored. I thought, for a moment that she was going to keel over. But she pushed past us at a walk, her head high despite her wheezing breaths.

A feral growl floated through the quiet night air and brought gooseflesh up on my arms.

I jolted to a stop, yanking Fair to a halt with me.

"What's wrong?" Rog asked, sounding irritated. "We're close enough to the bleachers that I can smell stale beer and sweat."

"Shhh!" I told him, my gaze raking the shadows that were thick around the edges of the stadium. After a moment, I risked a soft call. "Elvo?"

Another growl sifted toward us from the end of the stadium. A dozen yards away from the first one.

My goosebumps got goosebumps and had goosebump babies.

I made a sudden decision. Whipping around, I said. "You guys get to the press box and set the antidote up."

"What about you?" Fair asked.

I glanced around and felt my breathing quicken as the shadows began to shift and take form.

Ghouls. Lots of them.

I fought panic. I didn't see any ghouls in the press box area. Rog and Fair should be able to reach the top if I distracted the monsters on the ground. "I'm going to buy you some time. Now go!"

Rog pulled a short sword out of his pants and I stepped back. "Whoa! Have you lost your mind? You might cut something off with that thing in your pants."

He rolled his eyes. "I have a sheath."

"Of course you do. That's part of the original package," I told him, my tone dry.

"A *sword* sheath," he said in exasperation. "I'll help you fight."

An ugly picture formed in my mind of Rog being overcome by dozens of ghouls and I shuddered. "No. You need to help Fair."

His expression turned mutinous. "I can fight. Juggler's

been training me and Mols." He swung the sword, nearly decapitating me. "I'm pretty good with this thing."

Soft growling filled the air. The sound appeared to come from dozens of ghoulish throats. A ring of the bent, leathery monsters had broken free of the shadows and were on the field with us, lumbering closer at an ever-increasing speed.

"There's no time!" I wanted to shake him. "That antidote Fair has is our only hope. I need you to protect her. Get her up there and help her set up. You need to do this, Rog."

Rog's face had gone slack. If his skin wasn't naturally brown, he'd have probably gone white with fear.

I shook him gently. "Rog!"

He blinked and did the one thing I would have never predicted. He threw himself at me and clung tightly for a beat. I was so shocked at first that I didn't react. Finally, I patted his back a couple of times and shoved him gently away. "Go."

He nodded, looking tearful. "I'll tell Molls what you did for her. For the city." Then he turned around, grabbing Fair's arm, and they started running. Somehow Fair kept up, but she stumbled a few times.

Feeling as if I'd done all I could for the moment, I closed my eyes, took a deep breath, and gripped my weapons. A spit-filled snarl yanked my eyes open and I turned just in time to keep from being sliced open by nasty ghoul claws.

The thing launched itself at me and I ducked sideways. I lifted my blade as the monster sailed over me, slicing across its middle. The ghoul hit the ground and I quickly finished it off, straightening again just in time to suffer another attack. The monster hit me hard and sent me sprawling on the grass. The breath knocked out of me, I lay there for a beat looking out into a sea of pulsing red eyes and wide maws with misshapen, blackened teeth. The foul stench of the creatures was thick in the air and, surrounded as I was, it soon became overwhelming.

I said a silent prayer and rolled, jamming my gun between the legs of the first ghoul I hit. I fired. Even I winced as the thing screamed, the sound high-pitched and awful. It went crazy, running around with one arm flailing and the other holding its tattered family tree.

Crashing into the monsters around it, the ghoul gave me the perfect cover to roll to my knees and start crawling through the crowd. There had to be hundreds of the things. I would never make it out alive, unless I got really creative. I jammed my gun into the magic family box of the nearest ghoul and fired. Chaos ensued.

I shot to my feet and started running, slashing my blade from side to side as I ran. I didn't have time to aim for the lethal areas, there were just too many monsters. A single, persistent thought kept scrolling through my brain.

Move, fight, survive.

I slashed and fired and screamed as razor-like claws slashed deep. Fiery pain enveloped me from wounds in my arms, legs, back, and chest. One slashing claw nearly caught my throat, but I favored that ghoul with a trimmed family tree and moved on. I was coated in blood. Black blood from the ghouls. Red blood from me. I was starting to get concerned when the red overwhelmed the black.

My movements started to slow, my limbs growing heavy, and the world was beginning to spin around me.

I'd bounced several times, barely avoiding one predicament only to land in the middle of another. There seemed to be no spot where I could find a moment to breathe.

Fangs sank deep into my shoulder and I screamed. One leg buckled and took me to the ground on one knee. Smelling a victim, another ghoul ran at me. Out of instinct, I threw up my blade and impaled it, then I shoved my gun between my knees and shot the ghoul attached to my shoulder. As predicted, the monster let go of me and screamed.

Somehow I got to my feet, but I was swaying, weak. I was at the end of the line and I knew it.

A ghoul came at me and I kicked out, sending it flailing backward, and...down, down, down. It disappeared into one of the holes in the field King Henri's excavations had caused.

I fell backward, closing my eyes on a whirling queasiness, and accepted my oncoming death.

The night split on an eerie howl. And then another.

The ghouls jerked upright, the glow in their eyes pulsing frantically.

Unbelievably, they began to retreat.

I wanted to take a few more of them out, but I couldn't move. More howls filled the darkness, the sound eerie and way too close. When I was no longer surrounded by ghouls, I shoved to my elbows and looked around. Blazing red, yellow, and orange eyes glowed through the night.

The glowing orbs bobbed as if the owners were on the move. If I squinted, I could barely make out the immense, black shapes.

Hellhounds. Lots of them.

No, no, no, no, no! Not good!

A massive furry beast stepped out of the night and stood over me, eyes flaring above an enormous muzzle the outline of which I could barely make out in the darkness. The thing's huge teeth were so white they shone as if under a blacklight.

My heart throbbed a painful beat in my chest and, for a long moment, I feared I was going to have a heart attack. Then a string of drool dripped onto my throat, sizzling hot.

"Ow." Dog spit. Blech.

Using the sleeve of my shirt, I rubbed off the acidic spit and glared up at the hound. "Maybe don't drool on me when your spit is superheated."

The beast's tail wagged from side to side, his tongue lolling out of his grinning mouth.

That was when I realized there was a lot of screaming. I looked around and found the field engulfed in Hell fire. The hounds encircled the remaining ghouls and red and orange flames consumed their nasty forms with an efficiency I had to respect. Hell fire. "You brought friends, I see." A wet tongue speared my ear. "Ah!"

The big hound chuffed, his chest expanding a couple of times as he laughed.

I grabbed hold of Elvo's fur and used it to help me stand. Burning pain erupted all over my body. On an impulse, I wrapped my arms around his neck and gave him a hug. "You really saved my bacon on this one," I told him. "I'll even forgive you the wet willy."

Elvo chuffed softly and head-butted my boob, nearly knocking me over. "Okay," I said, stumbling backward. "Hallmark moment over. Let's go help Fair and Rog. We're gonna get rid of these big, leathery cockroaches if it kills me." Right on cue, I choked on an intake of sulfurous air and coughed, my chest tight under the hell fire smoke and pain flaring from a dozen wounds as I convulsed.

In that moment, I decided it likely would kill me.

When I could breathe again, I took off running. The first explosion happened when I was ten yards from the bleachers. It knocked me off my feet and sent dirt and grass into the air in a thick geyser.

20

I'M NOT GOING TO LIE...I MIGHT HAVE EATEN THE EAR

I lost track of Elvo as the dirt rained down on my head, and when I tried to call his name, I choked and fell into another coughing fit.

The second explosion hit me when I was trying to stand, flinging me back to the ground several feet away. I hit the ground hard and bit my tongue as agony ratcheted up my body.

I hadn't even gathered my wits before the third and fourth explosions lit up the night. I sat in the middle of it and blinked, all of my senses on overload. I couldn't even look for shelter. There was no time between blasts.

The big overhead lights came on with a metallic thunk and I squinted against the overly bright light. My eyes were no longer accustomed to light after being in darkness for so long. They watered and refused to open beyond a squint. Feeling around the grass for my weapons, I managed to come up with only rocks and dirt.

"Well, well, well," said a familiar, well-modulated voice.

I pushed off the ground and stood, swallowing blood. Like the ghouls around me, I swayed slightly as dizziness swamped me. "Henri," I said, my voice like broken gravel. "To what do I owe this exquisite pleasure?"

He chuckled softly, the sound oddly enhanced.

Forcing my eyes to open all the way, I found him standing near the front spectator entrance with another man.

I squinted at the tall, lean form next to Henri. A form that made the king of the ghouls look small and non-threatening. The other man had a thick cap of brown hair which was touched with gray at the temples. As I recognized him, I knew there would be gray strands threading through the brown, and sexy crinkles at the corners of the man's brown eyes. I'd watched him address the state and speak to the press many times.

It was Governor Treadcamp.

Behind Treadcamp were several bulky men. The governor's security detail stood with hands clasped and muscular legs in a wide stance. They all wore dark suits and had military-short hair. Had they been ghoulified too?

"Governor." I called out, inclining my head. "You might want to reconsider the company you're keeping these days."

The politician stared right through me, his mouth slightly agape and his expression blank. In a moment of stark horror, I realized he'd been marked. Suddenly everything fell into place. Henri had had control of the governor for a while. It was how he'd managed to lay siege to the stadium with minimal pushback from the police. And how the ghoul king had been able to get so far with his plans in such a short time.

"What's the game plan, Henri?" I skimmed a look around the field as I attempted to keep the king distracted with conversation. The ghouls I'd battled were nothing but char stains on the field, some of the spots still smoking. I relaxed a bit, seeing them gone. There were likely hundreds more below the ground. Maybe thousands. We weren't out of the woods yet. Not by a long shot. But every little bit helped. "The gig's up," I told Henri. "You can't possibly believe you're going to be able to camp out here indefinitely, creating your happy little monsters and being left alone."

Henri's grin was almost endearing. He had a cute dimple on either side of his cupid's bow lips. "Ah, but you see I won't be staying here at all. This was just a staging area...a testing ground. I'm ready to move into nicer quarters." He slapped the governor's back a little harder than necessary. Treadcamp swayed under the assault but his expression didn't change.

"Luckily for me the governor's mansion is very large, with lots of underground space for my minions. I should be very comfortable there."

Where had the Hellhounds gone? There was no sign of them anywhere. It was like they'd just melted away. Why weren't they dispatching Henry? Then I realized the flaw in that idea. They'd surely attack Treadcamp too. They'd attack anyone whose paths they crossed.

That would be bad.

I was suddenly glad they were gone. I just hoped Elvo had gone with them and wasn't lying injured somewhere.

"Now, lovely Rae. You'll need to come over here and accept your mark. It won't hurt much. And when it's done you and I can make special plans together. I like your spunk. Your drive. Of course, your loyalties are flawed. But all that will change once you're mine. Step it up, my dear. We have much work to do, and the city grows restless."

I snorted. "In your dreams, ghoul boy. If you want to mark me, you're going to have to take me by force."

He sighed. "Force it is, then. How tedious." He turned to

Treadcamp's men and flicked his fingers. As one, they moved forward, heading for me as they drew an assortment of weapons.

Well, I thought *That answered that question.*

The men pulled guns, blades, and batons from the hidden spaces in their dark suits. One of them pulled a couple of flashbangs from his slacks and I fought the urge to take off running. Glancing around, I realized the explosions had put me in the center of a small island of grass. Deep, jagged ravines surrounded me, the sides so steep and sharp with broken rock that they wouldn't be fun to navigate.

"What's with the explosions, Henri?"

His grin widened. "Just a little insurance to keep the humans from becoming too nosy. I've nearly gathered up everyone with any power, but there are a few who are still avoiding my special touch. They're threatening to bring cameras and equipment in to see what's going on with my little manufactured 'earthquake'." He looked inordinately pleased with himself and I couldn't help wishing someone would pinch his head off and end his reign of terror.

Movement drew my gaze toward three figures running my way from the bleachers. It was Molly, Justice, and Rog.

I cast a look up to the press box, where an orange-pelted head moved behind the glass. Fair was still working on the antidote. Hopefully, it would start going out soon.

I opened my mouth to yell at my friends to get the Hades out of there, but a thwuck, thwuck, thwuck sound, which I realized I'd been hearing for a while, grew close enough for me to identify. I tipped my head back and saw the lights of a helicopter overhead.

"Oh hells," I muttered as the chopper's blades pummeled me with wind and spun the dirt around me into tiny, annoying whirlwinds. I squinted and covered my face with my arms, suffering a barrage of tiny assaults as explosion debris pelted my flesh.

"Rae!"

I forced my eyes to squint open and I yelled to be heard over the noise. "Mols, what are you doing? Get under cover."

She didn't respond, only shielding her face and waving at the incoming aircraft.

Realization struck me. "You know that pilot?" I bellowed.

She gave me a long-suffering look. "Do you ever listen to anything I tell you?" she yelled.

"Of course," I yelled back. But as soon as I responded, I realized it was a half-truth. Since Molly's chosen profession was about as far from anything I cared or knew anything about, I did tend to block out about half of what she said. In my own defense, I'd been a cop for several decades, dealing with life-or-death issues. If I zoned out over how many zippers her new rural dancer pants should have, I figured I could be forgiven.

By me. Not by Molly. She'd never forgive me for being less than a hundred percent focused on her and her stuff.

"Don't you remember that photo-shoot in Montana last year?" she all but shrieked as the chopper came within ten yards of touching down.

My blank expression was apparently enough for her.

"Rae!"

"Sorry," I said, skimming the security ghouls a quick glance to see where they were. Fortunately, they seemed to be struggling to find a way to safely cross the ruptured ground around me.

In that moment, I realized that the condition of the field was going to create a more dire challenge. "Mols," I yelled. "Where's he gonna land?"

She pointed to a small corner of the field, near the

outfield fence. The chopper tilted, starting to swing around and head that way.

A stun grenade sailed over my head. "Down!" I screamed, jerking my gaze away and dropping to a knee as I covered my ears. The flash went off five feet from the nose of the aircraft, sending the helicopter into a spin as the pilot presumably got smacked in the retinas by the deadly flash. He managed to retain enough control to land the craft, but it was an ugly landing.

Hundreds of ghouls chose that moment to boil onto the field. Some of them came from inside the stadium. Some of them climbed like large spiders from the holes in the field.

Metal whined and screamed. I looked toward the spot where the chopper had gone down and grimaced as the ground gave way beneath it, the skids on one side dipping below the soft earth. The blades slowed and the engine whine cut off. As I watched, the pilot threw open a door and climbed out. Molly ran in his direction, jolting to a stop as she spotted the ghouls lumbering across the field.

"Molly!" I screamed. "Get back upstairs."

She looked at me and shook her head, her pixie face belligerent.

I bit back a swear. A deep, prolonged moan had me whipping around to discover that I was about to be joined on my little island by unfriendlies.

My blade was already slashing as the first monster climbed from a hole in the grass. The thing's head flew off and I kept swinging, beyond caring at that point about anything but killing ghouls. They'd twitched on my last nerve. I was over it.

Monsters started screaming.

My gaze slid toward Molly and Justice, finding them armpit deep in ghouls and fighting hard. Behind them, flames swept the edges of the field, and I lifted my panicked gaze to the press box high above. Fair's face was pressed against the glass. Her eyes looking like ping pong balls in her round face.

I glanced around, looking for the Hellhounds. Because they had to be there. I didn't see them. Human screams had me jerking around to find Treadcamp's guys backtracking toward the center of the field, surrounded by several ghouls. A couple of the security detail were bleeding from claw marks. Apparently the old ghouls weren't big fans of the newer models. It was a glitch in the system for sure. Hopefully one we could take advantage of.

"How's it goin' Kitten?"

I jumped and yelped in an unmanly way. Spinning around, I barely kept from beheading Tom before I realized it was him. My ex's face was pale and sweaty. His shirt was bloody where he'd been marked and the skin showing at the vee neck of his shirt was an unhealthy purple as if the wound had become infected.

I couldn't tell if he'd completed the transition to ghoul or not. Just in case, I took a couple of steps back. "Tom. What are you doing here?" Clutching my blade in a sweaty palm, I prayed he didn't attack. I really didn't want to kill the father of my child.

Two red-eyed ghouls climbed up onto my island and I opened my mouth to tell Tom to get out of the way. I snapped it closed. He wouldn't have listened to me anyway. He never had.

In the blink of an eye, he reached out and tore an ear off the first one, then kicked the second one between its leathery legs.

Both ghouls hit the turf, one dying and one writhing in pain.

To my horror, Tom eyed the ear for a beat and then shrugged, starting to lift it toward his mouth.

"Don't! You. Dare." I told him.

Tom frowned, then offered it to me. "You want it?"

I gagged. "No. Drop it. We need to get out of here." Unfortunately, the fire around the outside of the stadium was driving all the ghouls into the center. Where we were.

Heavy gunfire drew my attention back to the helicopter. The pilot, clad in a black Kevlar suit and holding a machine gun, stood on top of the downed chopper and was cutting down monsters with rampant glee. Next to him, her tiny body vibrating beneath the weapon's kick, Molly looked just as happy to be blasting ghouls into pieces.

I sighed. There'd be no getting her back to normal now. Next Spring's clothing line at The Muddle would be urban guerilla chic.

"Woof!"

I looked up as an enormous, shaggy hound lumbered my way. Elvo wagged his tail with unbridled enthusiasm before opening his maw and blasting two ghouls with Hell fire.

His tail never stopped wagging.

I turned back to Tom and caught him chewing. He stopped as soon as I saw him. "Gah! Please tell me you didn't."

"Um. I..." He shook his head. "I don't want to lie to you, Kitten. I might have eaten the ear."

I shuddered so violently, my teeth clacked together. "Stop calling me that." My stomach roiled. "Come on. We need to get out of here."

Tom kicked a dead ghoul into the nearest hole and leaped over it. I jumped too, barely making it to solid ground and rolling to keep from breaking something.

"Rae!"

I waved at Justice and took off running. The flames were growing and heat was making me sloggy. Sweat coated every inch of my skin and made my array of wounds sting. When I reached my partner, I carefully looked him over. "How are you?"

Justice's smile was warm and a little bit sexy. I mentally derided myself for even noticing with everything else that was going on. "We're good," he said. "Fair doused us before she started rigging the atomizer."

I gave Tom the gimlet eye. He shrugged. "It's taking longer to work on me. I guess because I was a monster for longer."

Hopefully he was going to regret that ear when he finally healed.

"How are we going to get out of here without the chopper?" I asked Justice. "The Hellhounds have lit up the entire fence line." I frowned. "Wherever they are."

Before Justice had a chance to respond, there was a commotion near the dugout. We glanced over in time to see a bunch of people pouring out of the space. My first instinct was to lift my weapons. But then I saw Juggler leading the onslaught.

I had only enough time to wonder which side of the taint line he was on before I found out the hard way where the Hellhounds had gone.

Hundreds of leathery, red-eyed monsters lumbered onto the field. Herded by a terrifying number of the hounds.

21

SHOOTIN' MONSTERS FOR POINTS

An eerie, blood-chilling howl traveled through the hounds, their fiery gazes flickering the colors of flame as they moved to encircle the entire field.

Justice and I went back-to-back, blades out, knowing even as we did that trying to kill that many massive Helldogs with blades or even guns would be like spitting into a forest fire to stop the spread.

Flames licked at the stadium seating, ate their way over the torn and rutted grass, and moved inexorably toward the downed chopper. I was happy to see that Molly and her friend had abandoned the aircraft and were battling their way toward us.

Then I realized she was moving toward Juggler. Panic flared in my chest. "Mols, no!"

I started to cut her off, but Justice grabbed my hand. "Let me go!" I growled, trying to yank out of his grip. "She needs to stay away from him. He's feral."

Justice shook his head. "Take a look at them. None of those people have the taint." I did as he suggested, though I was vibrating to get between Molly and the dozen or so people heading our way. He was right. They looked okay.

I glanced at Tom. "Go see if Fair is ready to let that stuff loose."

He nodded and took off running, his gait less plodding than before. Maybe the antidote was finally starting to work on him.

Molly reached Juggler and threw herself into his arms. He held her tight, burying his face in her neck.

I strode over, Justice at my side. "You'd better not be fixin' to bite," I growled at Juggler.

He raised his head and gave me his trademark grin, waggling his brows. "Maybe just a nibble or two."

I growled and Molly rolled her eyes.

Juggler lifted his short sword to indicate the people behind him. They were looking worriedly around the stadium, likely wondering how they were going to escape the flames, the ghouls, and the Helldogs. "All of these people are immune to the ghoul taint," Juggler explained. "We've been scouring the tunnels below to find as many as we could. The ones who didn't turn went into hiding, some of them getting lost in the tunnels before we found them."

I was happy to hear there was such a thing as immunity. "Is there a way out down there?"

Juggler nodded. "Yeah. Or...there would have been if those blasted hounds hadn't set the whole place on fire to drive Henri's monsters out."

"Has anybody seen Elvo?" Justice asked.

"He was here a few minutes ago," I said. "He showed up to save my bacon and then disappeared again. What's up with him, anyway?"

Justice grimaced. "There's something you don't know about Elvo," he told me, lowering his voice and guiding me away from the others. "He might be a mutt, but he comes from powerful stock."

"Okay," I said. "I knew the big stinky dude was a devilish kind of guy. How does that explain the fact that he keeps disappearing?"

Justice scrubbed his gristly jaw with both hands and made a face. "That's not exactly what I was trying to say."

"Maybe just spit it out then? My brain is fried and I'm about to topple over from pain and weariness."

"Got it." He cast one last look at Juggler's crowd. "His dad's kind of a big wig in Hell."

I felt my brows arch. "How big?"

"Hound General in the Hellhound Army."

I had no idea what that meant, but it sounded impressive. "And Elvo's what? Working with Pops to help get rid of the ghouls?"

"Yeah. Unfortunately, Pops isn't really too worried about innocent bystanders. He's kind of a grizzled old curmudgeon."

"Is that hound-speak for he chomps first and asks questions never?"

"Exactly." Justice grinned widely and parts of my body melted and yearned.

I found myself grinning back.

"So Elvo's had to walk a fine line," Justice went on. "He's got some discretion with the dogs but he doesn't have total control."

"He needs to get them out of here before they eat all the good people and the ones we're trying to save."

Justice nodded. "He's in Hell right now, trying to get that done."

"It's ready!" Tom bellowed from the press box.

I held up a hand. "The antidote is going out now. If

Tom's any indication, it will take time to do its magic. I guess we need to try to keep these guys corralled here until it's had time to work."

Justice nodded.

Movement in my peripheral vision dragged my attention that way.

A big black guy in a Kevlar suit approached, hand outstretched. "Rae?"

I looked up into a stern brown face that would probably be attractive without a dozen bleeding wounds. "That's me."

"I'm Hank."

I took the pilot's hand. "Hey, Hank. That was some pretty cool shooting you were doing up there on that helicopter."

He grinned and every bit of sternness leached from his face. "It was like being back at my favorite arcade again," he said. "Shootin' monsters for points."

"I had the most points!" Mols said as she joined us.

Hank looked down at her and ruffled her uncustomarily messy hair. "By one, Tiny. Only one. You wanna go back up there, I'll blast that score out of the water."

Molly blew a raspberry, her hazel gaze sparkling with pleasure. "You can try."

Hank laughed. "It's like hangin' with my baby sister again."

"Baby!" Mols barked. "I'm old enough to be your mother, soldier."

Hank's response was to rub the top of her dark head with his knuckles. She squealed with outrage and punched his arm.

"Hey!" Rog said, jogging up to us. "Fair's coming down."

"Good. Is the antidote rolling?"

"Yeah," Rog said. "But so are the ghouls. Our babysitters just left."

My head jerked up and my gaze slid around the field. He was right. The hounds were gone.

And hundreds of ghouls were turning their sights on us.

Sweet cherubs on a crescent moon.

I sighed, tugging out my 9mm and a full magazine. Ejecting the empty mag, I slammed the fresh one home. I glanced at Justice. "I found one of your fan blades along the way. I lost it again though."

He nodded, holding up his hands. "I've got spares." Sure enough, two more of his special weapons filled his hands.

"Good." I jerked my head toward Juggler. "Does the mob over there have weapons?"

The ghouls started to move. Hank lifted his machine gun. "I've got a full weapons locker on the bird. Send them my way."

I nodded. "Thanks, Hank."

"I'll tell them," Molly said, and took off running.

I sighed. Too weary for words. "I guess we're doing this again."

Justice stepped closer. "I guess so." He stood inches above me, his warm breath bathing my face and doing funny things to my libido. Again, I couldn't believe I could react to him when surrounded by ghouls. I guessed we had a special kind of relationship. Twisted and weird.

Justice lowered his head and hesitated, his lush lips a breath away from mine. We hung there for a beat, lost in our own little world. Then Justice said, "Rae?"

I pulled Justice-scented air into my lungs and slowly released it. "Yeah?"

He tensed. "Duck!"

I ducked, and his blade cleaved the air where my throat had been, neatly slicing the head off a ghoul with its claws in the air ready to attack.

"Thanks," I said, feeling breathless.

"Oh," he growled sexily. "You're welcome." Quick as a cobra strike, his warm lips found mine and then he was spinning away, in full-out battle against three more ghouls.

I whirled on my heel and went back-to-back, my blade making short work of another five ghouls.

The air in the center of the field erupted in smoke and Elvo trotted out of the haze, his big body coated in flame. All around him, ghouls went up in flames when he looked at them. For the first time, maybe because of what Justice had told me, I had a healthy respect for the big goof. He was really pretty darn scary.

Juggler's crew launched themselves into battle with a cry of what sounded like sheer excitement, blades slashing and slender, well-toned forms dancing around their prey. I realized they weren't just Average Joes. As I took on a wave of slavering monsters who'd become easier to kill since I'd learned their rhythms and weaknesses, I eyed the men and woman in Juggler's group, noting the muscled limbs and the confident way they moved. A tattered uniform told me one was a cop. No, at least four of them were cops. I speculated that others were military and a couple appeared to be security, wearing the stained and tattered remains of once-white dress shirts, and sporting super-short hair. Maybe some members of Treadcamp's detail hadn't succumbed to Henri's poison.

And speaking of Henri...

Glancing back to the spot where the king had stood with the governor, I realized they were gone. The governor's tainted detail was battling it out with some of Justice's people, a fight that seemed evenly weighted on both sides.

As I watched, one of the suited guys stumbled and fell to his knees without taking a blow. With instant understanding, I realized what was happening. As his opponent wound up for the killing slice, I screamed, "No! Don't kill the baby ghouls!"

When the woman who'd been about to finish off the security guy looked my way, I pointed toward the press box, Where Fair stood holding the atomizer, a silvery cloud of antidote spewing from it.

Fortunately, Juggler must have explained to his people, because a look of understanding spread across her face. She nodded, and moved into protective mode around the downed guard rather than trying to finish him off.

As if a switch had been flipped, baby ghouls all across the field dropped, unwounded, to the ground. They'd been the last to be infected and were the first to be cured.

Which created another problem.

Monsters didn't need a score card to figure out that some of them had changed sides. As soon as humans started to lose the taint, they became victims of their mindless, flesh-eating nest-mates. And they were helpless, writhing on the ground as the antidote burned the last of the taint from their bodies.

"Protect!" I screamed, swinging at a particularly aggressive leathery guy as he tried to move into my protected zone. Apparently a veteran of the ghoul wars, the thing ducked my slash and leaped on top of me, driving me to the ground and pinning my legs and arms with gore-coated claws.

The ghoul lowered its pointed head, sharp teeth clacking together inches from my throat.

I struggled to release an arm so I could shoot my gun. The thing was too strong and I was bone weary. Grave-scented spittle hit my face and claws pierced my pinned flesh. I couldn't do a thing to stop what was coming.

I was losing the battle.

In sheer desperation, I slid my finger to the trigger of my 9mm and fired. My angle was bad. I hadn't really expected to hit anything important. Which was why I was shocked when the monster stiffened, its glowing eyes going dim, and fell on top of me.

"Good shootin', Tex," Justice said. He kicked the ghoul off me and grimaced when he saw where I'd wounded the ghoul. "Ouch. Remind me not to irritate you overmuch."

I lay there panting. "I didn't think that would work."

Justice shuddered. "It worked." He shuddered again. "You're terrifying, Rae."

I grinned. "Nicest thing anybody's ever said to me."

A shout went up and I closed my eyes. "Now what?"

He looked toward the sound of yelling and slowly smiled. "Now, we finish off the dregs." He offered me a hand. "It appears the good guys are winning."

I let him pull me to my feet and stood there swaying wearily. Taking stock of the field, I realized Justice's assessment was spot on.

In the outfield, Hank and Tiny Rambo stood in the center of a large pile of dead ghouls, their machine guns fairly smoking from overuse. Rog stood next to Molly, his short sword dripping thick black blood and his clothes and face coated in the stuff.

Go Rog! I hadn't thought he had it in him.

Around Elvo was a sea of charred flesh and soot marks in the churned grass.

Juggler and his crew, including the reclaimed humans, were working their way through what looked like about thirty ghouls. Hundreds more lay dead around them.

I couldn't believe it. "We actually won."

Justice dropped a warm, heavy arm around my shoulders and tugged me close, placing an exuberant kiss on my temple. "Listen Rae. Let's agree that you won't ever tell anybody about me on that ledge, okay?"

I grinned up at him. "I don't know. That seems like important information."

He sighed. "What's it going to take to keep your mouth from flappin'?"

I thought about if for a beat, though I already knew what I wanted. "Three bottles of the magic healing balm."

He frowned. "One bottle."

I shook my head. "Four bottles. And that's my final offer."

He tugged me close with an arm around my neck. "You drive a hard bargain." His lips dropped to mine and I melted into pure sweet deliciousness that didn't last nearly long enough.

"Rae?"

I turned to find Fair standing a few feet away, her ruddy cheeks probably pinker than before she'd witnessed our kiss. "Um, we're not done," she said, her gaze skittering away from us as if she was embarrassed. "Henri has compromised a lot of the city. I need to return to Aere and get more antidote." Her voice broke and I suddenly remembered.

Anil.

We needed to save the Director of the Travel Bureau and the governor. And probably much of the police department, the EMTs and other hospital personnel, and likely thousands more. I was suddenly beyond exhausted.

"Right." I gave her an encouraging smile. "Do you know where Anil is?"

Her eyes glistened with unshed tears as she shook her head. "No. But I can find him. And to save the rest, we need a better dispersal system."

"What are you thinking?"

Her gaze slid to the downed chopper.

"Ah." I grinned. "Let me go talk to Hank. Justice, can you give Fair a ride home?"

"It would be my pleasure."

"You'll need to watch out for the guy with the jelly bullets," I warned him. "You do *not* want to get hit with one of those."

Justice frowned, mouthing, *jelly bullets*?

"I'd like to hear the plan first," Fair said, crossing her arms over her chest. "It might affect how I spread the antidote."

"That's a great point. We need to take out Henri," Mols said. "Or he'll just keep poisoning the people we save."

I frowned. She wasn't wrong. We could spread all the antidote Fair could get around Fort Wallace, but if Henri kept making monsters as fast as we could cure them, we'd lose everything in the end anyway.

"Does anybody have an idea how to do that?" Rog asked.

"First things first," Fair said, a stubborn tilt to her chin. "We need to save Anil. If he's compromised, all the dimensions are in serious danger."

I nodded. "I have an idea how we can kill two ghouls with one blade," I said.

Fair looked alarmed.

I flapped a dismissive hand. "Metaphorically speaking," I clarified. "We need to do a press conference."

Her eyes went wide. "What? Why?"

I smiled. "Henri's a king. At least in his own mind. The thing about people who think they're important is that they can't resist getting in front of a camera and talking about how wonderful they are."

Molly nodded. "That's true. But how does that get us

Anil? He's been tainted. He's not going to do or say anything except what Henri tells him to."

"Exactly," I said. "So, we need to give Henri a reason to include Anil in the conversation."

They all stared at me as if I were speaking Greek.

Hank scrubbed a big hand over his face. "Do you need me to spread the antidote, or not?"

"We definitely do," I said. "So, here's how it's going to go."

22

AND TO WHOM AM I SPEAKING?

J uggler, Justice and Hank were working on getting the chopper out of the ground and back into flight.

Molly was in makeup...her face folded into a frown as she tugged on the ugly flowered dress and eighties style wig we'd excavated from the remains of the storage room inside the stadium. Her pixie face was all but lost beneath the auburn helmet of "big hair" and the flared skirt of the dress hung well below her knees, too long by a foot on her petite frame.

Her diva stylist was bug-eyed as Molly harangued him, his skinny frame lost in the folds of the dress as he tried to find a way to make it fit.

Finally, one of Juggler's rescued cops, no doubt tired of hearing the constant bickering, marched over to them and grabbed the bottom layer of the dress, his arms bulging as he gave the fluttery finish a quick rip, tearing it from the rest of the dress. That small adjustment left Molly and Rog goggle-eyed for a beat before they burst into excited chatter. The newly reduced dress fell to just above Molly's shapely knees, making the oversized white belt at the waist look stylish instead of just outdated.

"Okay?" the cop asked, his dark gaze sliding appreciatively over Molly's legs.

She gave him a thumb's up and everyone expelled a sigh of relief. At least until three minutes later, when Molly and Roger started fighting over Molly's makeup.

"I look like a circus clown," Molly yelled.

"The cameras will strip normal makeup from your face," Rog screamed back. "It needs to be overemphasized."

"Since when are you a camera expert?" Molly growled out.

"Since I helped with about a thousand fashion shoots of your stuff," he responded.

Molly stilled, her mouth falling open. "Oh. Yeah. That's right. Okay. But don't make me look like Raggedy Ann."

I snorted. With the big red wig and the perfectly round spots of color at her cheeks, she totally looked like the beloved doll.

Both sets of eyes snapped to me. I felt their joint irritation like a bolt of lightning to the solar plexus. Lifting my hands in a defensive maneuver, I backed slowly away, my gaze locked on the two rabid fashionistas.

At least we'd figured out why the clothes had been in the stadium. Tom had overheard Henri telling his minions it might help his creations fit in better if they dressed in "normal" clothes. Unfortunately, most of the stuff the clueless minions had gathered was decades old and would have made Henri's designer ghouls stick out like broken thumbs if they'd worn them.

"Ma'am?"

I swung to face a cop, a woman, who I knew to be one of Juggler's people. She wore a badly-fitting uniform that had been cobbled together from the dregs of several cops' unis so she would be presentable enough to deliver our message to the governor's office. "Did you deliver the invitation?"

She nodded, tugging at a too-tight shirt. "I told Tread-camp's secretary."

"Did she seem coherent?"

The cop understood my question. Henri's baby ghouls looked normal, but he didn't seem to have mastered the art of making them walk and talk like real people. He'd likely figure that little nit out given enough time. But we didn't intend to give him that time.

"Yes, ma'am," the cop responded. "The secretary had been crying and looked scared. But she promised she'd give the invite to Treadcamp."

Which meant she'd give it to Henri, whom I had no doubt was sitting at the governor's desk. "And the news orgs?"

"Invitations delivered. They were loading vans when I left."

"Great. You know what to do?"

She nodded. "I'm on Team A. We're crowd control. Team B is under cover in case we need to use force."

"Perfect. Great job."

The cop jerked her chin in acceptance of my praise. But a shadow clung to her dark gaze. I knew how she felt. Every-thing was riding on our little ruse working. If we failed, Fort Wallace would be only the first of many cities to fall to Henri's deadly schemes.

I gave the woman a smile. "Someone brought food and coffee in... bottles of water. Get something to eat and drink and then get into position. The action will start soon enough."

I watched her stride quickly toward the front gate, which

was open, the chain hanging uselessly to the ground. The uniformed officer was built like a colt, all long legs and narrow hips. I'd been built like that once. A few decades previous. But I didn't regret my womanly curves. Not anymore. Not really. I was strong and healthy. And I mostly liked myself. A woman in her fifties couldn't really ask for more than that.

A husky cheer went up behind me. I turned to find Justice and Juggler slapping palms. The copter began to rise off the broken earth, bobbling from side-to-side as the buried skid found its way to open air.

I yelled for Fair. But she was already hurrying in that direction, one of Treadcamp's reclaimed security guards carrying two of the ugly atomizers alongside her.

I slid my hand into my pocket and fingered the cylinder resting there, hoping against hope that Fair had known what she was doing.

That our plan would work.

The plan was coming together. Within an hour or so, we should have Henri in our grasp and Anil safe and sound. Then we'd heal the rest of the city. And I could finally wash ghoul goop off my clothes and body.

Maybe I'd even eat a little something before I fell into bed and slept for a week.

EVERY NEWS ORGANIZATION within a fifty-mile-radius of Fort Wallace had shown up for the press conference. Everybody was interested in the strange plague that had taken over the city. As well as the "earthquakes" that had turned a key portion of the downtown area into heaving hunks of dirt, grass, and rock, dragging some of it underground.

The press conference had been billed as providing key information about the causes, the solutions, and the future of Fort Wallace. If the invitations intimated that Governor Treadcamp had information about the entire state...well... it might not be a lie. If we didn't stop Henri in Fort Wallace. He'd surely keep spreading his poison near and far until someone did stop him.

The prospects for the state, country, and world grew worse with every area he conquered. Every individual he poisoned.

Despite the direness of our situation, the mood was almost festive, with members of the media running around getting the first available pictures of the mess that had once been Wasp Stadium. Like the insatiable culture vultures they were, the press scanned the area with enormous video cameras, while on-air reporters gleefully spouted terrifying stories of potential devastation and destruction.

Speculation about the governor's special guest had the crowd humming. Behind the thick wall of news media, regular people stood with pale, pinched faces, hands nervously twining as their worst fears seemed to be verified.

I shoved itchy fake hair off my face and slid my gaze over the rooftops, finding Hank and the helicopter sitting on the roof of an old brewery building that had been turned into a restaurant and shopping venue. Like every other business in the cordoned-off part of the city, Food Alley, as it was called, had been closed for days. The chopper should be fine there until it was time to take the antidote on the road. Nobody was looking up. Not when there was so much to worry about right in front of them.

"The governor's here!" someone shouted in an excited voice.

I turned with the crowd to see a black limo easing slowly

up the street. The windows were, of course, darkened and I couldn't see who was inside. With any luck, Henri took the bait and brought Anil along to show that he was on top of things, not only on a local but on a worldwide level. But, if he didn't bring the director with him, we could always get to Anil later. Once we had Henri under control, it would be easier.

Even as I had that thought the sense that we were missing something and it would all go horribly wrong assailed me. I'd been fighting that feeling all day long. So much so that I was starting to worry it would be a self-fulfilling prophecy.

The limousine pulled to a stop next to several police cruisers and waited. As cameras flashed, no one climbed out of the car. Nothing moved.

The crowd started to murmur and, as the moments passed, called out to Treadcamp, trying to entice him from the car. Anger rang through the shouts as more time passed without movement, and my surety that things were about to blow up in our faces grew with every shout, every static moment that passed.

Then, one of the limo's doors opened. A huge man in a dark suit climbed out of the front passenger seat and walked around to open a back door. Henri climbed out, his feral gaze sliding immediately around the crowd. I lowered my head and stepped back into the shadows of an ambulance near the podium.

For a tension-wrapped moment, the king's hostile gaze locked on a spot too close to where I stood, as if he knew I was there. As the moment stretched, I tensed to leap out of the shadows and tackle him to the ground. It would be better to move too soon than to lose the opportunity altogether.

I was on the razor edge of moving when Henri finally smiled, turning to wave at the assembled crowd.

A second door opened and Treadcamp climbed out, his trademark smile firmly in place. He lifted a hand and waved at the crowd and cameras flashed all around as his constituents clapped and called greetings. Treadcamp had been a very popular governor, as evidenced by the immediate cessation of hostility as he moved toward the podium where Henri already stood.

Molly, a.k.a. Raggedy Ann, stepped smoothly toward Henri with a big, old smile on her painted face. I grimaced when I spotted the big red dots on her cheeks, hoping Rog knew what he was talking about. If Mols was caught on national television looking like a child's antique doll, she was gonna castrate him with her sewing scissors.

"Hello, Governor," Molly said in a too-high voice. "It's such a pleasure to have you here today."

Whistles and calls from the crowd seemed to support Molly's sentiment.

Treadcamp nodded at Molly and kept smiling, the curve of his lips horribly similar to a death grimace. Apparently Henri had managed to teach his puppet only one expression.

"As we told you in our invitation," Molly went on. "News 56 out of Portfield wishes to get to the bottom of what happened here at the beloved Wasp Stadium. We feel that people have a right to know." She winked at Treadcamp, earning herself the same rigid and uncomfortable grin. "And you're just the man to tell us."

Apparently tired of being ignored, Henri gave a confident, warm laugh. "Hello, Ms...?"

Molly gave the king a simpering laugh. "Tiffany Glass, News 56. And to whom am I speaking?"

I rolled my eyes. Molly wasn't exactly nailing the whole dumb news gal schtick. But it was good enough, I supposed.

I tightened my hand around the cylinder in my pocket and took a step forward, my muscles bunching in preparation for a sprint.

"I'm Governor Treadcamp's new medical consultant. I'm here to clarify what's going on in Fort Wallace." He frowned as a guy in a dark suit ran up and whispered something into his ear. Henri glanced at Molly and nodded. He gave her a broad smile. "I'm sorry, Ms. Glass was it? I'm not familiar with your station. Where did you say you were from again?"

Molly's smile looked slightly strained. "Portfield. Just outside of Evansville. We're a small market." She spread her smile around the crowd, winking saucily. "But we're hungry and News 56 was the first to request information about what was going on here in Fort Wallace. I predict we're not going to be small for much longer."

A few cheers went up and a couple of wolf-whistles. Amazingly, Molly actually had the crowd firmly in her grasp when Henri, reluctantly, it seemed, nodded and smiled. "I've been consulting with a seismologist who works around the world," he told the crowd. "To understand both the ruptures in the ground here and the gases they seem to have released."

"Who's the seismologist?" a reporter asked helpfully. "Can we speak with him?"

"I'm afraid Dr. Anil can't speak to you today. He's with our rapid reaction team working up a solution to the poisonous air the breaches are emitting."

Henri's words had what I assumed was the desired effect. People jerked back and started murmuring, their gazes flying to the open gate and the broken stadium beyond. The crowd started to turn on their heels and walk briskly away, covering their noses and mouths with their hands as they fled.

Henri smiled, his feral gaze filled with amusement.

Molly sent me a panicked look. I glanced toward the chopper and raised my hand, giving them the "go" signal.

The blades of Hank's helicopter started to spin.

Henri started to glance that way.

I moved, lunging toward the podium.

The man from the limousine reached for Henri, no doubt planning to spirit him away.

Her expression irate, Molly lifted her microphone and Rog screamed, "Mols, no!"

But it was too late. She struck Henri in the head and the guy in the suit jumped on her, carrying her to the ground.

Chaos burst around us.

Cameras flashed. People screamed. Our people jumped into action, battling back a fresh wave of Henri's security who appeared out of nowhere. But worst of all? Ghouls bubbled from the surrounding buildings and rose straight up out of the ground. Hundreds of them, their red eyes glowing with a special kind of fervor. Unless I missed my guess, they were some of Henri's oldest minions. And they would be the hardest to kill.

Sweet cherubs on a blood-red moon.

Things had gone nipples-up in a big way.

23

NOT A CHANCE, DOUG

The helicopter dipped low over the street and a pale mist spread from it to fall over the combatants. I could just barely see Fair's round face and even rounder eyes through the mist, which had a clean if fairly antiseptic smell that wasn't at all unpleasant.

I was vaguely aware of shouting, screams, and the sound of weapons being fired as I sprinted after my target.

Henri was being quickly spirited away beneath the umbrella of chaos around him. I couldn't let him escape. He was the biggest target out there and the one most likely to slip through our fingers if I failed to do my job.

The biggest thing in my favor was the fact that Henri only had one guard at the moment. Unfortunately, that one guard was a big guy—a wall of muscle on a frame that was well over six feet tall—and he was strong enough to nearly carry Henri toward the waiting limo.

Acting out of sheer desperation, I pulled out my 9mm and shot at the tires of the big car, then did the same for any other vehicles nearby.

The big guard stopped, spinning around to put himself between me and Henri, and started firing.

Even his gun was big.

45-caliber bullets pinged off the boxy form of the ambulance and I ducked, my gaze locked on target as I hit the ground and rolled beneath the vehicle. Stretched out on my belly, I fired at the guard, aiming for his legs.

Blood blossomed just above his left knee and he barely twitched, shoving Henri toward the limo while still firing at me.

I rolled out from under the ambulance and kept firing.

Out of the corner of my eye, I saw Justice making his way toward the limo. He was on the other side of it with his blades out. His eyes met mine and he gave me a slight nod.

My palms sweated around the cannister I held as I nodded back, then took off running.

Henry's security guard had reached the limo. Opening the door, he shoved Henri inside.

Justice leaped onto the hood and threw himself at the guard, blades slashing. The two men rolled off the side of the limo and jumped to their feet, fists swinging and blades slashing.

For a big guy, the guard was fast and agile, barely seeming concerned about the fact that he'd lost his gun and was facing Justice and his blades.

I scurried past them and grabbed at the limo's door.

It was locked.

"Henri, open the door," I said in a pleasant tone. "I don't want to kill you."

Henri snorted. "Right. You just want to be friends."

I grimaced, "Maybe not friends. But, something. How about, amiable enemies?"

The car shifted slightly and I realized Henri had moved

into the driver's seat. I couldn't let him drive away. Even with three flat tires, the car would likely last long enough for him to escape with me on foot.

I took a running leap onto the hood of the car, my gun pointed right where Henri's head would be. I could see the shape of his head and shoulders behind the darkened glass. "Don't do it, Henri."

A gun went off and agony sliced across my shin.

My leg buckled and I went down, the cannister I'd been clutching flying free of my hand.

"Jeezopete!" I screamed, throwing myself to one hip and sliding off the car. I hit the asphalt hard and pain slashed down my spine, yanking the breath from my lungs.

I lay there wheezing for a beat, fighting to push to my feet. But the cumulative hours of stress, strain, and life-threatening abuse had taken their toll.

I really just wanted to lay there a while and try to process my pain.

The door nearest me opened and two small feet in shiny shoes appeared beneath it.

Still wheezing, I lifted my gun toward Henri. He grinned down at me. "You know that gun won't kill me."

I pulled the trigger, but Henri moved fast-fast and the bullet slammed into the car door. Before I could fire again, he kicked at my hand, sending the weapon flying.

His smile was creepy, like the stretch of dead lips over a desiccated face. He knelt beside me, lifting a long black fingernail toward my face. "It won't be so bad, lovely Rae. You and I can be best friends once you take the mark." He ripped my shirt away from my shoulder and lowered the nail to my skin. Agony burned through me as he sliced his mark into my flesh. The touch of his nail was like acid against my skin.

He slashed the final line across the mark and his nasty grin widened. "There. Now you're mine."

Weakness took my limbs. A mental fog slid through my mind. I tried to get up but my body wouldn't obey. The mark was already working.

Henri looked up at the big man who appeared near my shoulder. "Carry her. We need to go."

Hot tears slid down my cheeks. Was Justice dead? I shook my head from side to side, trying to deny what had to be true. If the man he'd been battling was still standing, Justice had failed. They wouldn't walk away leaving him alive.

The man bent down and tried to scoop me up. I found one last bit of resistance, my fist punching him in the nose as my other hand flailed to get beneath me. My fingers touched the cylinder and it slipped away.

"Quit messing around Fifty-Five. Pick her up and let's go."

Apparently Henri wasn't even letting his victims keep their names. As well as being turned into nasty death monsters, they being dehumanized with numbers instead of names.

The man punched me and my head slammed into the ground. My awareness dimmed, turning charcoal around the edges, and I was suddenly hanging over the man's shoulder.

Henri climbed into the limo and the man tossed me onto the seat facing the king's.

He backed out and closed the door.

Outside the limo someone grunted. Something heavy hit the door and the car shook.

I bit my cheek to keep myself from fading into unconsciousness. I needed to help. I needed to...

Henri leaned closer, still looking smug. Whatever was going on outside, he clearly didn't feel threatened. "What was that, lovely Rae? Did you say something?"

I fought back a wave of dizziness and smiled at him, blood coating my lips. "I..."

Henri moved closer, his expression taunting. "You?"

I lifted my left hand, fingers closed in a loose fist.

He laughed. "What are you going to do, Rae? Punch me?"

I grinned. With his attention on my left hand, I lifted my right hand and slammed the object I'd been holding into the side of his neck. His eyes went wide and he fell backward on his seat, gasping. His fingers clawed at his throat as he turned to leather before my very eyes.

The door flew open and Justice looked in at me, then slid his gaze to the quickly dehydrating king. Henri had started to turn to dust, a pile of gray dirt growing where his feet had been, "It took you long enough," he teased before scooping me up and pulling me out of the car. "I can't believe you were just lolling around in there while I did all the work."

I snorted, laying my head on his shoulder as a cool, soothing mist filtered over us, pulling the fog from my mind. "If you hadn't played so long with your food, I could have netted it out much faster."

Justice snorted. "Okay, Rae. If you say so."

"I do," I responded, unable to stop the smile that wanted to stretch across my face. "That's exactly what I'm saying."

~

THANKS TO FAIR'S super-charged antidote, the mass of remaining older ghouls soon joined Henri in the literal dustbin of history. I snorted at the thought, determined to find a way to sneak that into a conversation with Justice. Just to see if he laughed.

Between Teams A and B, Hank's Rambo-like machine gunning as he flew over the field of battle, and the rest of our people kicking ghoul backside, we managed to extinguish a large number of the monsters before the antidote even did its thing.

"You got Henri?" Molly asked, coming up behind me.

I turned around, yelping and dancing backward when I spotted her. She frowned. "What?"

Her crazy wig was globbed over with black blood, the weird flips on the ends staunchly still standing despite the sheer weight of ghoul goop coating them. Her face was smeared with the stuff, and her weird cotton dress? I grinned. "I'm picturing you in a redo of the Carrie movie."

She grinned back at me, posing with her oversized microphone and her short sword. "We'll call it Molly."

"Of course," I laughed, resisting the urge to give her a hug.

"What's so funny?" Rog asked. Molly and I turned to him and we both yelped. Rog was... Well, Rog was...

"Ugh," Juggler said, as he slid his gaze over them both. "You two sure are a sight."

Roger looked at Molly and jumped back. "Ah!"

I laughed at the indignant look on her bloody pixie face. "Hey, war is heck."

"Spoken like a hard-core soldier, Molly-bug."

She slid her smile to Juggler, her perfect white teeth all but glowing in her gore-coated face.

"They're like the father and daughter in the gothic American painting, if the father stabbed all his neighbors with his pitchfork," I said.

Everybody looked at me, frowning. "What? You don't get the reference? You know those sour looking people in front of the farmhouse?" I shook my head. "You all are seriously lacking in classical learnin's."

Justice snorted and threw a warm, heavy arm over my shoulders. He leaned in and kissed me on the head. "Don't we have one more victim to save?"

I slapped my forehead. "Anil!"

"I've got him," Fair said.

We turned to find her heading our way with a smile on her ruddy face. Elvo trotted alongside. Anil trailed them slightly, looking gobsmacked but non-ghoulish. His stocky body was covered in dirty and tattered clothes and his combover had failed, the long hairs sticking up all over his balding head.

"How'd you find him so fast?" I asked as Justice slapped Anil on the back, nearly sending him to the asphalt.

Fair gave Elvo a pleased glance. "I asked guide Elvo to sniff Anil out for me. I figured Henri would have him nearby in case he decided to trot him out during the press conference."

Anil gave her a look that was hard to read. For an uncomfortable moment, I wasn't sure he shared Fair's affection the way she seemed to think he did. "I was in that old brewery building with hundreds of nasty ghouls," Anil said, shuddering violently. "I'm never leaving Aere again."

I dropped an arm around him. The little man's head barely reached my shoulder. "Trust me when I tell you that staying home isn't all it's cracked up to be."

"Ma'am?" a deep male voice said. The man who'd walked up to us was one of the governor's security detail. Actually, he was one of Juggler's people who'd been immune to Henri's mark. "Governor Treadcamp would like to thank you personally for getting rid of Henri."

I twitched, realizing I'd completely forgotten about the governor. Team A had been in charge of scurrying Treadcamp to safety during the kerfuffle, but I'd been too busy trying to take out Henri to notice if they'd succeeded. "He's okay?"

The man smiled for the first time since I'd met him. "He's a little groggy. Tired. But he's very grateful to be out from under the ghoul king's influence."

I nodded. "I'd be happy to speak with him, but he can address all of us," I said. "We were a team. No one person did more than another."

"Well, technically, you were lying on the ground drooling on yourself while I fought the biggest security guy I've ever seen before, but...potato, potahto." Justice said.

I smacked him on the arm. "I was *not* drooling on myself."

"If you'll all come with me?"

We followed the security detail toward a new limo that was idling near the curb a block away from the stadium. As we approached, the back door opened and Treadcamp himself climbed out, the ghost of his trademark smile appearing briefly as he nodded at us. "I just wanted to thank all of you for what you did. You saved this city maybe the world from a deadly attack."

My team lowered their heads and shuffled their feet. Nobody seemed comfortable with the praise.

Treadcamp stepped toward me, his hand outstretched. Not wanting to be rude, I took it. "Raelynn Kitt. I understand I owe you special thanks for saving my life." He sandwiched my hand between both of his, the skin warm and smooth.

They were the hands of a man who worked behind a desk rather than with his hands.

I ran a hand through my messy auburn hair, knowing it was probably a cap of wild tangles after over twenty-four hours of fighting and fleeing. "We were just doing our jobs, sir."

He cocked his head slightly, his eyes narrowing. "Well, you went above and beyond." He lifted his gaze from me and looked around the group. "All of you. For your efforts, I'd like to offer each and every one of you unlimited free meals in any of the restaurants in Fort Wallace for an entire year."

"Does that include the bars?" someone called out and we all laughed.

"Not unlimited, no." the governor said. "But I'll buy a round for all of you as a special thank you."

The group cheered, clearly a bunch of cheap dates. I personally didn't drink, but I'd use the heck out of that restaurant offer.

Treadcamp waved at them and then touched my arm. "May I speak with you for a moment, Rae? I can call you Rae?"

"Of course," I said, allowing myself to be drawn away.

He stopped in front of the open car door, reaching into his shirt pocket and pulling out a card. "My personal cell is written on this card. Please call me if you ever need anything." His gaze heated, smoldered. "Or if you just want to talk. I'll always take your call."

My cheeks warmed at the innuendo in his words and tone. "Um. Thanks." I lifted the card and slipped it into the pocket of my jeans. I expected the governor to climb into his limo and leave, but instead, he reached out and gently clasped my hand. "I could always use someone like you in my security detail."

Warmth bathed my back and a familiar, scintillating scent surrounded me. A heavy arm dropped around my waist and Treadcamp lifted his stare to a deep-set sapphire gaze, which was currently filled with hostility. "Ah. Well," he said, nodding toward Justice. "Remember what I said, Raelynn."

Justice's arm tightened as Treadcamp climbed into his car and it pulled quietly away. "What did that snake want?"

I turned a smile to him. "Me, apparently."

When Justice's hand bunched into a fist on my hip, I laughed. "He offered me a job on his detail. Apparently, he could always use someone like me." I waggled my brows.

Justice grunted. "I'll bet he could."

"Let's go home," Mols said as she joined us. "I'm making breakfast for everybody, and then I'm going to bed for a week."

Juggler appeared in a timely fashion, his gaze bright with good humor. "Now that's an offer I can't refuse." He danced his brows at Molly. "You weren't thinking of actually sleeping were you?"

We headed for the spot where we'd left Rog's car. Hank, Rog, and Elvo fell in with us.

I had no idea where Fair and Anil had disappeared to. They'd probably gone back to Aere. Or Tom. The last I'd seen of him he was yarking in the bushes, the ear probably coming back to haunt him.

"Stop being such a lech, Juggler," Rog said, interrupting my thoughts.

Molly laughed. "Considering how I look right now, I'm a little impressed he's even considering what it sounds like he's considering."

After all the battles, the street was dark and eerily quiet. The silence rubbed against my nerves and made my steps quicken.

"Call me Doug," Juggler said. "I'm no longer juggling women." He tugged Molly under his arm. "I'm a one-woman guy now."

Molly snorted. "Who's the lucky woman? Nobody here asked to be exclusive."

Juggler nuzzled her ugly wig. "Come on, Molly-bug. You know you want to."

"As long as we're getting names right," a deep voice said from the back. I turned to find Hank grinning. "Her name is Tiny Rambo."

Molly laughed with delight. "TR for short."

Elvo woofed in agreement.

With a throaty click, the street lights snapped on again. Only a few of them around the front stadium gate remained dark. Their bulbs shattered in the fighting.

My nerves settled under the scalding illumination, which pushed the shadows back until I no longer worried that something nasty hid within them.

"I'm not sure I can date a Doug," Molly said, her pixie face folding into a frown.

"Now TR," Juggler said good-naturedly. "A name is just a name."

"A good name is a good name. And Doug just sounds too much like an accountant. Or a dog groomer."

"Both good and reputable careers," I said, ever the diplomat.

My comment earned me raised brows from Justice. "Is this a good time to tell you my real name is Bruno?" he asked.

I barked out a laugh. "No. There's never a good time for that."

"Oh!" Rog said ahead of us.

"Oh?" we all echoed. We stopped next to Rog and our gazes followed his, "Oh."

Rog's car was no longer sitting where we'd left it. To be strictly accurate...it was sitting *under* where we'd left it. The car had been eaten by a sinkhole.

I patted Rog on a skinny, gore-stained shoulder. "RIP underpowered girly car."

Rog shook off my faux comfort with a glare.

We all stared at the little boombox of a car for a moment. I sighed. "Uber?" I suggested.

"Nobody's going to give us a ride looking like this," Rog whined. We scanned a look over ourselves and then started to laugh.

"Come on," I told them. "We'll go to my place. It's only a couple of blocks away."

Or a mile. Potato, potahto.

"I call dibs on the first shower," Molly said.

"We should double up to save time," Juggler said, his brows dancing.

Molly indulged him with a grin. "Not a chance, *Doug.*"

"Do you have any food at your place," Justice asked dubiously. The man had clearly figured out my grocery buying—or not buying—habits.

"I've got cheese and bread. If nothing else, you can char up a few dozen sandwiches in the fireplace." He'd done just that once before when I'd been laid low with magic poisoning. Being from an entirely different dimension, Justice had had no idea what to do with my stove. Camp fires he understood. And my wood-burning fireplace looked like a camp fire to him.

Elvo had enjoyed the hunk of charcoal I'd slipped to him when my sexy guide hadn't been looking.

"Woof!" Elvo agreed happily. At least one of us would get some food.

The End

DON'T MISS OUT

ABOUT THE AUTHOR

USA Today and Wall Street Journal Bestselling Author Sam Cheever writes mystery and suspense, creating stories that draw you in and keep you eagerly turning pages. Known for writing great characters, snappy dialogue, and unique and exhilarating stories, Sam is the award-winning author of 100+ books.

To learn more about Sam and her work, visit her at one of her online hotspots:
www.samcheever.com
samcheever@samcheever.com

ALSO BY SAM CHEEVER

If you enjoyed **Bouncing Toward Ignominy**, you might also enjoy these other fun books/series by Sam. To find out more, visit the **BOOKS** page at www.samcheever.com:

Midlife Muddle Paranormal Women's Fiction

(For more adventures with Rae and the gang!)

Mature Magic Paranormal Women's Fiction

Enchanting Inquiries Paranormal Cozy Mysteries

Yesterday's Paranormal Mysteries

Reluctant Familiar Paranormal Mysteries

Country Cousin Mysteries

Silver Hills Cozy Mysteries

Gainfully Employed Mysteries

Honeybun Heat Series